It's All Love

A Novel

By Howard Storm

2012

Table of Contents

Chapter   Page

Chapter 1 - Coming Home   .   5
Chapter 2 - The Renaissance   .   14
Chapter 3 - Softly and Tenderly   .   21
Chapter 4 - Lightning Strikes   .   29
Chapter 5 - The Visit   .   34
Chapter 6 - All You Need Is Love   .   39
Chapter 7 - Back to School   .   45
Chapter 8 - Soup and Sandwiches   .   51
Chapter 9 - Charity   .   60
Chapter 10 - Unlocked   .   68
Chapter 11 - Down, but not Out   .   75
Chapter 12 - What is Truth?   .   82
Chapter 13 - The True Church   .   90
Chapter 14 - The Best of Times   .   97
Chapter 15 - The Big Event   .   105
Chapter 16 - Belize it or not   .   112
Chapter 17 - Finding the Maya   .   122
Chapter 18 - Re-entry   .   130
Chapter 19 - The Crash   .   138
Chapter 20 - Fall From Grace   .   146
Chapter 21 - The Hope   .   154
Chapter 22 - All the Time   .   162

Chapter 1 - Coming Home

When Dan opened the door he saw an almost empty house. It was like the day they had moved in twenty-three years before. A place that had been a home was now just a structure with a few items scattered about. This had been a home to his family filled with joys and tears, but now was as bleak as a tomb. He was reluctant to enter. There was a shock dragging him into a slow motion time as he shuffled through the barren rooms. On a table without chairs was a note attached to a manila envelope. The note said to read the papers, sign then, and return as soon as possible. The papers inside the envelope were the settlement agreement that his wife had drawn up with the advice of an attorney. There were self sticking notes in the places he was supposed to sign and date.

The only good thing was the dog. She was beside herself happy to see him. Mindy was a seven year old golden retriever and she was his dog. Mindy loved everybody with unconditional love but Dan was her man. It took a few minutes to register the leaping barking dog in the foreground of emptiness.

Dan was like the recipient of a flash grenade and was having difficulty recovering reality. Thirty-six years of marriage gone just like that.

While Dan had been in China concluding the biggest deal of his life, Donna had the moving van loaded to begin her new life free of him. This was all done in secret plans that had begun months before to avoid conversation. She had been planning this for a very long time but he was not aware of the depth of her feelings of contempt toward him, largely because he loved her very much. He had ignored the signals. He was in denial that they would ever separate.

Question bombarded Dan's mind. How can you invest your entire life into loving a person and have them completely reject you? What is there to life other than giving love and being loved? If

5

the person you love with all you have to give doesn't want it, is there anything left to live for? These thoughts and darker ones started spinning out of control in his head. Many voices were speaking on top of one another shouting for dominance in a cacophony of self destruction. Thoughts of self annihilation kept leaping into the whirlwind. Details of how to accomplish the deed haunted him. There was not going to be a failed attempt to fall into oblivion, rather this was going to be a coup de grace that would leave no possibility of failure.

One problem that interrupted the planned journey to nothingness was the constant interruptions of the dog. Mindy kept interjecting, "Hey boss, you want to go for a walk? Want to play? Got anything to eat? Do you want to rub my ears?" This was the only contact Dan had with the world and she was needy. Even when he tried to ignore her he couldn't turn her away for very long. It was as if she knew more than a dog could possibly know and was doing everything she could do to let Dan know he was needed. If the spirit of love can be mediated through a dog then Cindy was pulling out all the stops.

For days Dan isolated himself from the world because he didn't want to hear advice or be given platitudes from well meaning friends. He walked in the woods with Cindy and asked himself and the universe the same questions over and over again. It all came down to one simple question. What's the point of living? The universe gave no answer.

After a couple of weeks of isolation he was at the supermarket, out of necessity, getting supplies when he came upon an old friend named Peter whom he had not seen in years. To avoid talking about his situation he asked Peter about how his life was going. To his surprise Peter had also been abandoned, but that had been years earlier and he was doing much better and even had a wonderful wife and family. Dan was thinking, "Well how nice for you but it will never work out for me." And Dan was also thinking he wasn't going to be around in the world much longer anyways. Peter could see that something was terribly wrong with

Dan and he gently kept asking questions about how his life was going. He learned enough and was perceptive enough to know Dan was in deep emotional trouble and was doing his best to hide it. Dan was not as good an actor as he thought he was. When Peter sensed he had hit the wall with Dan and he was getting really defensive, he stopped the conversation. The spirit of compassion which had been working in Peter for some years inspired him to do something that he was reluctant to do. Peter said in parting there was something that had seriously changed his life. He had a new set of friends who met regularly to talk about things and he would like Dan to come with him next week to meet these people. Dan thanked him for the offer but he wasn't interested in being around people just now. Peter asked him to think about it and he would contact him soon to see if he would give it a try.

During the next few days Dan rode an emotional roller-coaster from the pit of despair to a few rare moments of elation. He tried getting drunk one night which only made him more depressed. He tried to invest himself in his work which was bringing in some income. He attempted contact with his wife but she insisted that he speak only to her attorney. He was careful to not let anyone know about his plans for committing suicide because he didn't want them to intervene. He tried reading but he couldn't concentrate. He thought about an old high school friend who had become a Catholic priest and got so far as looking up his number in the phone book, but he didn't make the call. So he walked this narrow ledge between afraid of the gaping blackness of death and the almost unbearable burden of being alive without hope, purpose, or love.

Then one evening Peter showed up and was gently persistent that Dan come with him and meet with his new friends. It was not far, Peter would drive, and if he wanted to leave at any time Peter would take him home. Dan didn't want to go, but it seemed to mean so much to Peter that he finally gave in just to keep from hurting his feelings.

It was raining hard during the fifteen minutes it took to get to the meeting. There was little conversation and the time was filled with the metronome cadence of the windshield wipers. This gave an air of expectancy to the ride, but good or bad was the expectancy. "What am I doing? What am I doing?" kept repeating to the beat of the wipers in Dan's head. When they pulled up to a house there was a big jock like guy hunched under the entry way to the front door trying to keep out of the rain while he pulled hard on a cigarette. "Sorry man, he said, trying to quit but not much luck so far." He pitched the smoke and followed them indoors. There were a dozen men sitting around the room in an odd assortment of furniture. The mix of dining room and upholstered living room chairs was more homogeneous than the mix of ages and dress of the men. Different ages, different dress; from well-worn work boots to highly polished dress shoes, and blue jeans to three piece suits. Dan was anxious about what he was getting into but relaxed by the diversity of the group. He would not be conspicuous by his casual attire. When the chatter subsided the leader of the group, named Frank, introduced himself and asked everyone to do the same. After the introductions Frank explained that this was a Christian support group. Dan learned later some of the men were members of Hartwell United Methodist Church and some belonged to other churches and some attended no church. Frank explained they had certain rules for the hour discussion and he proceeded to review the rules. There was to be no dominating of the conversation by any one individual, there would be no judgment of anyone, no one had to participate, no one was to give advice to anyone, they were there to speak what they needed to share with the group, and they were there to listen. Dan was feeling comfortable with these rules, particularly liked the part about no participation. This is precisely what he had in mind.

Then the bomb dropped. Frank said he would begin with prayer. Everyone dropped their heads and closed their eyes except Dan who was not about to trust them that far. Frank began to pray, "Heavenly Father we come together tonight to be in your presence and to listen to one another and to hear your Spirit speak to our hearts. We are all broken and have gone astray from the right ways, your ways, and your love. Help us be whole as you are Holy. Heal our broken minds, hearts, spirits, and bodies we pray in the name of our Savior Jesus the Christ. Amen" Then all the men enthusiastically in unison said, "Amen."

Of course Dan was silent and dazed. He had stopped praying when he was a teenager and he couldn't recall ever hearing a prayer like that before. There was no poetry or Elizabethan English anywhere in the prayer. But even more striking than the simplicity was the sincerity in which it was spoken. He wasn't sure if that counted as an official prayer because it was so direct and unembellished. Whatever it was, he didn't care because he didn't pray or even believe in anything. He took pride in his moral superiority of not being a hypocrite by participation in rituals that no one really believed in and could never actually validate as truth.

Sharing began with an emotional intensity. It was hard for Dan to know whether to look at the speaker or to look away in embarrassment for them. These guys were pouring out the deepest secrets of their lives to each other. One man talked about his ongoing struggle with alcoholism, another talked about not having sex with his wife in three years: another man said he had begun attending church but didn't know if he believed or if he was just trying to convince himself, someone talked about cheating on his wife; one man had been unemployed for two years and was living off his wife's income at a job she hated; and one could barely speak at all for the tears and sobbing. He had trouble talking about his depression and uncertainty if he wanted to live. Every one who spoke tore down another brick in the wall Dan had erected between them and himself. When the man talked about his suicidal thoughts his words penetrated right into the core of Dan's being. Dan felt tears running down his face, and he was afraid and embarrassed others would notice. When he looked around he saw he was not alone in his tears.

The most amazing thing happened during this powerful emotional sharing. Although it was emotionally draining, there was an inexplicable sense of peace and well-being in the midst of these torments. Even though no one gave advice and no one commented on another person's story, some of the burdens were lifted in the process of speaking the truth to each other and in the presence of something that was in that room which Dan could not identify. It was as if there was someone in that room and men were being strengthened.

"What's going on?" Dan wondered. One side of Dan was ready to panic and run, and

The other side wanted to be a part of this openness and trust. He was not alone in his despair. These guys were living with the similar kinds of pain Dan had.

When the hour was over, Frank asked they join together in the Lord's Prayer. Dan had a moment of panic because he had forgotten the Lord's Prayer decades ago. Surely he would stand out as the only one not reciting it, and they would know he was not one of them. When they began some said the words loudly and distinctly while others mumbled so he followed along with the mumbles while listening to the words of the loud speakers. There was a strange familiarity to that prayer he had learned as a child. He wondered where he could look it up and study it someday. Maybe it would be on the internet. A huge "Amen!" followed the prayer and everyone started to buzz with chatter. A few men went out of their way to greet Dan. Surprisingly they didn't ask him questions even though he had shared nothing. He expected them to at least ask him why he was attending their group, but all they wanted him to know was that he was most welcome.

The time was coming for people to leave. Everyone was bumping into furniture in the crowded room, to get to each other to hug and say goodbye. This was very difficult for Dan because he wasn't a hugger. He tried not to show his revulsion with these displays of affection. What a relief when Peter said, "Let's go."

The ride home was awkward because Dan didn't know what to say. He was conflicted in his heart and mind. Finally, Dan asked Peter, "Since when did you become a Christian?"

Peter responded, "In some ways I'm just beginning, but I guess you could say a couple of years ago when I asked Jesus into my life."

Dan asked, "Is that when you started going to church?"

"No. Actually I have been attending church for a little over a year. I asked Jesus into my heart after reading the Bible because my life was a mess and I was looking for answers."

"Well, did you have a big experience with angels and all that stuff?"

"I had a big experience but I can't really describe it. It was more like something came into the center of me and has never left."

"What came into you?"

"Let's just say it gives me love, hope, peace and faith in the person of God."

"God is a person. That's news to me. When I took philosophy in college we discussed God, but the idea God is just a person is not very impressive."

"God is beyond comprehension and God chose to reveal His true nature to us in the person of Jesus."

"So you think Jesus is God?"

"I know He is God!"

"How do you know that?"

"The same way you are going to know Him. You ask Him and then you wait for Him."

"I doubt that's going to happen. I don't even know if God exists. Honestly I seriously doubt it so you are really wasting your breathe on me with this religious stuff."

"This is not about religion. We are talking about having a relationship with God."

"I thought you were talking about Jesus?"

"They are the same thing"

"Whatever."

Dan was getting agitated and wanted out of the discussion. So he changed the subject.

"They looked like a bunch of normal guys, but when they talk they sound like they're a bunch of losers. I mean their lives are messed up. Too bad whatever you believe isn't working for them."

"You don't know them well enough to call them losers. They trusted that group to speak about the doubts, fears, mistakes, and sins in their lives. Some of those men are highly successful. They were not there to try and impress anyone. They are....."

Dan interrupted, "That's for sure. They were not trying to impress. Depress would be more accurate."

"Did the meeting bring you down?"

"That the weird thing I am feeling better. Must be misery loves company or something like that."

Peter responded with his heart because his head told him not to say what he was about to say. "Dan, God was with us in that room."

Dan rapidly thought of several sarcastic responses, but chose to let them go. There was something in the room, but he wasn't close to identifying it as God.

As they approached Dan's house Peter said, "I'm very happy you came with me tonight. And I think you will have a better understanding of what happened in the next few days. Just remember you can ask Him anything for yourself, but you have to be willing to receive the answer. If you want to know what Jesus said about himself and God, read the book of John."

"Where do you get that book?" Dan asked in all seriousness.

"It's in the Bible. Do you have a Bible?"

"Yea, sure I have one," Dan assured Peter but was not so sure if he still had one. He was given one in Sunday school at his church when he was a child but where it was he had no idea. That was decades ago.

They parted company neither very clear about where the other stood. Dan didn't know that Peter was praying for him and very soon all the men in the group would be praying for him. The Holy Spirit had work for them to do and they were willing.

Chapter 2 - The Renaissance

That afternoon Dan was dying. Not physically dying; rather, he was ready to let go of the ego consciousness that had taken him to the precipice and was urging him to fall into the void. He was certain there was nothing after death, but he was close to believing it was preferable to life as he knew it. Cindy, the golden retriever, kept pulling him back, but she was fighting a losing battle with the dark voices in his head. They screamed there was nothing to live for in the world. While the Christian support group had previously broken their demonic grip on him, and the prayers of the men were still needed. When the evil one is fighting and losing, it fights harder. Dan knew nothing of the supernatural war raging around him except that he sensed something, and was in the center of chaos. One deep strong voice kept up the mantra, "Do it! Do it! You coward, do it!" In the midst of this barrage Dan reviewed his life and convinced himself of something he had never considered before. He now knew he has been responsible for the fate that had become his bleak existence. He had been equally responsible for the alienation and separation between him and his wife. He was responsible for only having friends that were only there for the good times. He was responsible for the distance that had grown between him and his parents and siblings. Only he was responsible for the maniacal obsession with his business that now meant almost nothing to him. All the possessions, prestige, and power were just an illusion signifying nothing but an ego trying to prove something to anybody in order to validate his existence. He had made these choices to love things over people. He was the one who saw humans as pawns to be manipulated around the game board of life. He had thought of himself as a winner and the people who viewed life differently were losers trying to justify their inadequacy to compete in the game of success.

Dan had lived the American dream and had prevailed. You only had to look at his net worth to see what he had accomplished by himself. The superman stood on the cliff and was painfully aware that he alone had chosen this course to this destination. He stood in the woods and cursed God. He screamed his rage at the Almighty whom he denied existed. He let God have it with both barrels of anger and torment. The woods were silent. He crumpled to the damp ground and wept. He tried to remember the Lord's Prayer but could only patch pieces together. Two pieces of the prayer he knew meant something important to him. "Forgive me my trespasses and deliver me from evil." That was genuine. There is no redo button in life. He could only regret how he had made so many bad choices, and there was no way to change it. The image of Jesus came to him. It was the Jesus in the print of the Good Shepherd that hung in Sunday school classrooms in thousands of churches. "Jesus. Jesus. Jesus, if you are real, help me!" he bellowed through his swollen throat into the stillness around him.

The rustling of the leaves and branches became music unlike anything he had ever heard before. There was a harmony and a beauty to the music that was amazing. He opened his eyes and the late evening sunlight filtered through the trees and it became brighter and brighter. White light more brilliant than lightning. The light almost consumed the trees and leaves, and what remained was a lattice work of gothic design in shining gold. This vision was superficial compared to what was happening inside Dan. He was filled with a peace that surpasses all understanding. This was much more than an absence of turmoil. This was a tangible presence of wholeness. He remembered being held by his mother as a child, but more intense. In fact the intensity of the peace was making Dan weep like he had never done in his life. Then a love so intense followed the peace. Dan was aware there is no language that can begin to describe this feeling of unconditional love. Dan knew he was beginning his life anew from this moment forward. He said aloud, "Jesus." The love intensified. He was surrounded by it. There was no time, or there was all time. He wasn't sure how long that experience lasted, but it eventually came to an end. He wished it would never end.

Gradually Dan stood up in the forest alone and got his bearings. He made it back to the house and began a frantic search for a book that had been put away decades earlier. There were boxes of books in the attic from childhood and college. He had a large collection of books from his early interest in philosophy. He had even considered being a philosophy major for awhile. That is how he had become an existentialist. He had moved from Friedrich Nietzsche to Albert Camus, and then on to Martin Heidegger. He learned under the guidance of his college professor to support the world view of nihilism and hedonism. That worked well for him in the competitive culture of corporate America. There was no god but self. The prevailing popular culture supported his philosophy.

He remembered his intellectual odyssey as he rummaged through the boxes of books looking for the book he had never read. In the bottom of one of the last boxes he opened he found what he was looking for. This thick book had an ox-blood red, cardboard cover with faded gold letters called the Holy Bible. The pages were printed on thin paper but in good condition since it had never been used. As he examined it in the dim light of the attic he came upon a handwritten inscription on the first page. The handwriting in blue ink was beautiful the way people were once taught penmanship. It was from a long-forgotten Sunday school teacher Mrs. June Easterly, who had presented this Bible to him. He tried to recall her face. It came to him in a dreamlike fashion. A vivid memory suddenly filled his mind. He saw himself sitting in a classroom singing "Jesus loves me this I know for the Bible tells me so." His heart ached for the child of innocence who sang those words and meant them. He wondered how was that hope lost over time? The abusive father, the hypocrisy of the church, the temptations of the flesh, and the craving to be his own master had all pulling him away from faith in God. It had been a gradual process throughout his adolescence. Without any spiritual influences in his life and religion appearing to be only a display of rituals that were meaningless to him, the lure of cynicism was greater than the mysteries of the faith. Even the movies and popular books revealed clergy as frauds supporting his unbelief. All the smart people he gravitated toward in the university were cynics and belittled religion. "Jesus" had become an oft repeated empty curse word without any meaning.

That funny little tune kept dancing through his mind. "Jesus loves me..."played over and over. He didn't know if this was true. He remembered one of the things Peter had said to him the night of the support group, "Read the Bible and ask Jesus if He is real." He climbed down the attic stairs. He sat in the new recliner he had just purchased a few days before and opened the book. Lots of strange names topped the pages, like what people named their children a hundred years ago. Then near the back of the book he came upon John. Maybe this would make sense, so he started to read The Gospel of John. Years later he realized this was no coincidence that he started with the Gospel of John, because the Spirit of Christ had led him to that place to answer the question about the authenticity of Jesus. "In the beginning was the word." And after four paragraphs he went back to the beginning and he read it again, and again. Now you can read the Bible and never get anything out of it, but if you are sincerely seeking God to speak to you from the words of the Bible it speaks to you. He was listening to God speaking to him. When he got to "And the word became flesh and lived among us." He said aloud, "Jesus." The book had spoken to him. He knew that it was so, even though he didn't know much, he knew that Jesus was the One. This was his first step in a journey that was the beginning of a new life.

Dan considered himself a rational man, and it was disconcerting that he had accepted something as true that he could not verify. The only evidence that he had was his emotional response to the words of the Bible. He wondered if he was losing his mind. He knew that his feelings had led him to all of the major decisions in his life. Some choices had been disasters and some were his greatest successes. He realized there were consequences to his decision to trust Jesus but he really had no idea what those consequences would be. Since his interior life was a shambles, he decided to test Jesus. He hoped he might experience again the peace and love he had experienced in the woods. The risk in believing Jesus is the Word of God was minimal, he thought to himself, because this was his secret and he was not about to talk about it with anyone.

For the rest of that day he read the rest of the Gospel of John and he reread many portions. The miracles intrigued him, he wondered if whether they actually happened. He concluded that if Jesus was God, then those miracles would be possible because there would be no limit to what he could do if he chooses to do it. One part that troubled him were the last words of Jesus on the cross when he was dying, "It is finished." What did that mean? He couldn't get a handle on why Jesus said that. What was finished? Did he pronounce himself dead? That made no sense. Since he didn't understand why Jesus died on the cross it was not possible to know why Jesus said what he did. It is finished.

One thing that intrigued him was the doubters and scoffers who appeared in the story. There was for instance, Nicodemus, who questioned everything Jesus said to Thomas who refused to believe unless he touched Jesus' wounds himself. Dan related to their doubting and was relieved that they came to believing in Jesus the hard way just as he had.

Peter called a few days later to ask how things were going. Dan didn't want to tell what had changed in his life over the phone so he asked if they could get together. That afternoon they went for a walk in the woods with the dog. Mindy was elated to show off to a new person in her milieu. Mindy was running around and looking for squirrels to chase up trees. Dan was cautiously describing what had transpired the past few days since they had last met. Peter just listened and affirmed Dan's experience. As they were deep in conversation they came upon a doe no more than forty yards away. Mindy smelled the doe before she located it with her eyes and took off after a worth prey. She had never caught anything in her life but this was an irresistible chase. The doe stepped over fallen logs with grace and bolted through the brush without effort. Mindy disappeared after her, barking her delight at the pursuit. The doe and Mindy quickly disappeared into the woods. Dan called and called for Mindy. She was truly gone. Dan began to worry about his beloved dog.

Dan asked Peter his question about Jesus saying, "It is finished."

Peter knew it was not appropriate to give a long discourse on atonement so he gave a simplified answer. "Dan, he died on the cross for you. He took your sin as his own. Even though he had never sinned he became your sin and took the consequence of sin which is death and died for you, instead of you. Jesus took your place on the cross. You could say he took the bullet meant for you."

This puzzled Dan, "I wasn't alive then."

"But Jesus knew you then, and he knew me and everyone who ever will be."

"Why would he do that for me?"

"That's just it, isn't it? Why would the Son of God do that for you or me? My friend, this is the amazing part of this whole business. God loves you that much that he sacrificed himself so that you would be saved from sin and death."

"What is he saving me for?"

"Not saving you for something. He is saving you from something. He is giving you eternal life, he is giving you a new heart and a new hope."

Dan confessed, "This is a lot to process. I've been reading the Bible. In fact I read the whole book of John. Some of it practically speaks to me, and I get it. Other parts are… well, the point is some I don't get, but I will. This is heavy stuff. How long did take you to understand it all?"

"I'm still working on it."

The light was beginning to fade as they headed back to Dan's house. There was no sign of Mindy. They called her name, but there was no response. When they arrived back at Dan's house they hoped to see Mindy at the door waiting for them. She had been gone a couple of hours now and this was not like her. Peter proposed they pray for Mindy's safe return. Peter said the prayer and Dan agreed. Peter left. He told Dan he had to go. Dan turned the front porch lights on to help Mindy find her way home. Not long after Mindy returned covered in burrs. She was wagging her tail because she had a most excellent adventure chasing the doe. Despite the fact it was going to take an hour of brushing to get the burrs out, Dan was filled with joy at her being found. His joy was compounded in heaven, because what was lost had been found.

Chapter 3 - Softly and Tenderly

"One day at a time," became Dan's new motto. He had picked that up while attending some AA meetings many years before when he was struggling with too much alcohol in his life. Unfortunately he could never convince the person in his life that really needed AA to attend. The support group he had visited with Peter was in some ways like an AA meeting. People in the group were being completely honest and letting the Spirit of God do the healing. The group soon became an important part of Dan's life and he rarely missed a meeting.

Five members of the group were going to take a getaway weekend camping trip to the Red River Gorge of Eastern Kentucky. Mark was a High School science teacher and an avid camper; he planned the trip, and invited Dan to go along. He was excited. He had always heard great things about the gorge, but had never taken the time to go there. He had not been camping since he was a young man and three days in the wilderness of the Kentucky Mountains sounded like a fun adventure.

When they arrived at the Red River Gorge State Park, they went to a primitive campsite called Coffee Creek. They set up their tents and Jimmy suggested they go for a hike before it got dark. They had a little more than an hour of sunlight left. Dan never imagined the gorge is such a dramatic place. There are limestone cliffs hundreds of feet tall surrounding a gorge that has several waterfalls and a beautiful river running down the middle of the narrow gorge. Dan was comfortable following the men who knew the trails through the Gorge. It was fortunate to have experienced men leading the hike since the trails are unmarked, and after a few miles it all looks alike. It would be easy to get lost in this forest. The sky was only visible to Dan directly overhead when he was down in the gorge enclosed by massive rock formations and deep forest.

Matt and Peter were engaged in a deep conversation about faith. Dan was listening to them intently. For Dan talking openly about his new faith in Jesus Christ was something new. All the men in the support group were eager to engage in conversations about faith. They were cautious about pushing Dan into going to church and were convinced that he would go when he was ready. They were aware he was being transformed by the Holy Spirit in studying the Bible and prayer. This weekend camping trip would be church for all them. "Wherever two are more are gathered in my name," said Jesus, "there I shall also be." The presence of Jesus is was what they experienced when they got together.

Dan soon discovered there are no level trails in the Gorge. He found himself either climbing up or down, and he had to watch his footing with every step. The tree roots and boulders are constantly reminded him to pay attention, and pick up his feet. The experienced men keep up a brisk pace which frustrated Dan because there were so many places to stop and behold the glory of the creation. Dan thought about the infinite complexity of all the wonders that were around him, and remembered how he had foolishly dismissed the underlying intelligence that made all of this possible. How could a serious rational person dismiss the majesty and complexity of the creation to a random bunch of accidents? He thought to himself. Yet, he himself had subscribed to that notion as the absolute truth of pseudo science. It dawned on him that this one just one more symptom of the prideful worldly philosophy before he experienced and knew there was more to the world than just his ego. Denial of any concept of God had allowed him to be his own god, which made him the Supreme Being. He had felt so superior to those who believed in a supernatural force that had been the source of all that is. His notion of the universe had changed one hundred and eighty degrees. Now he saw everything in the way he had belittled. He laughed inside himself.

Mark was walking beside him and noticed the broad grin on his face and asked him, "What was so funny?"

Dan confessed, "I use to think I knew everything and now that I know how incredibly stupid I was, I don't know much at all."

Mark was curious and inquired, "exactly what are you talking about?'

"I mean. Look at this place, the trees the cliffs, the river, and even you and me. Did all of this just happen by accident? I don't know how or why it is, but there is more than an accident! That is so obvious. You don't have to be a genius to see that there is more to this world than meets the eye. I do not know what God is or even understand anything about God, but I know there is something bigger than me, and it is behind or beyond all of this. Don't you think so?"

"I have always felt there is something that I call God," Marks said, "but the more I know about God the more I know I know so very little. The weird thing is the more you realize you don't know the more you get it. I teach science, but it science is always changing and it does not have all the answers. The problem is we are very uncomfortable with mystery. So faith has to accept certain things as mysteries. God is the first mystery, except what God has chosen to reveal to us about God's self."

"Is that why they call it blind faith," Dan asked?

"No. In fact," Mark said, "faith is not blind. Faith is just the opposite. Have you ever heard the hymn, "Amazing Grace?" It says, "I once was blind, but now I see." Faith opens your eyes to a far greater reality than you ever imagined. When you get Jesus in your heart you see more and farther than you ever did before. You start to see the world through Jesus' eyes."

"But in our materialistic culture," Dan said, "they think religious people are crazy. But I get what you're saying because in the past few weeks I am seeing more and experiencing more of the world than ever before. You know it is really like I was blind, but now I see."

The path was getting steeper as they climbed the shorter route back to Coffee Creek campsite. In the pinkish light of evening dusk the Gorge became a magical place. They had encountered so few people during their hike it seemed as if they were almost alone in the gorge. They were oblivious to the eyes that had been following them.

When they got back to the camp Dan pitched in as the men got busy making preparations for dinner and bedding down for the night. The food had been left in the cars parked by the road a few hundred yards away. Mark, the experienced camper, knew it was not advisable to leave food lying around in a wilderness area. They hung the remaining food in bags high up in the trees to keep it safe from critters. Dan was thrilled to see Matt had brought heavily marbled rib eye steaks which were cooked over a wood fire on a grill George had brought. The melting fat in the steaks made the fire blaze. In addition to the tender steaks, there were baked potatoes wrapped in aluminum foil, coleslaw, and pumpkin pie. It was about as good as it gets. The hike had given everyone a ravenous appetite. A few of the guys drank a couple of beers and others had tea.

After dinner the conversation changed from one topic to another until the conversation turned to the most embarrassing things that have happened in church. For example Matt told about the time he was the scripture reader in a Good Friday evening service and he had eaten some nasty hamburgers and onion rings before service. He described in graphic detail his discomfort with extreme gastric indigestion while he was trying to read the passion of Christ. The men found this hilarious but agreed their wives would not have approved of such accounts. George, who was a singer in the band at his church, told of what happened after church when he forgot to turn the wireless microphone off when he was scolding his son. There were many more such tales. These stories, Dan thought, may have seemed sacrilegious to the stuffed shirts he associated with church-goers, but actually were testaments to men who took worship very seriously. Dan was relieved to find these church goers were able to laugh at themselves, and didn't pretend to be holier than thou people.

Eventually they made their way to the tents and climbed into the sleeping bags. That night as Dan went to sleep he asked God to show him if these men were real in their faith or if they just talked a good game. While Dan had never trusted religious people, these men seemed somehow different to him.

The next morning after a big breakfast of blueberry pancakes cooked on iron skillets and cowboy coffee George suggested they shower in the waterfall they had passed during the hike the day before. When they got to the waterfall George and Matt decided the water was too cold for their comfort. The spring fed stream that fed the waterfall had not been warmed by the sun and it was the temperature of deep down in the ground. Mark, Dan, and Peter stripped down to their birthday suits and tried to wash in the frigid water falling off the cliffs overhead. Their skin was turning pale blue in the icy water. George and Matt were laughing at the timidity of the bathers when suddenly they went silent. The bathers didn't notice at first what was wrong with their friends. One by one they saw what was alarming their buddies. A group of rough looking men had approached. These good old boys appeared to be hunters at first, but they were a different breed of hunters because they were carrying automatic weapons with good size clips locked in place. Peter was a serious hunter and noticed these men were not your typical sportsman. They guessed correctly they were poachers and not to be messed with. Peter knew poachers live outside the law and do what they please.

There were a few tentative greetings exchanged when one of the mountain men picked up a pair of new hiking boots belonging to one of the bathers and started to make a grand show of admiring them. The rest of the mountain men were stone faced. The strangers secretly were enjoying the extreme anxiety of the naked men in the waterfall afraid to move and getting colder by the minute. They were just curious and having a bit of fun with these city boys. The man examining the boots dropped them to the ground. After both parties stood staring at each other for a while the mountain men walked away back into the forest. Dan and his friends were real quiet for a long time and then George whistled the tune to the movie "Deliverance." That made them as silly as a bunch of schoolgirls. They admitted they were terrified. They had felt very vulnerable. Some of them were shaking, but they pretended it was from the cold hiding rather than fear. They put their clothes on without drying off. George said, "You know they were poachers?"

"It is not even close to deer season. And it's not turkey season either," Peter responded.

"I was sure you were going to lose your new boots," George said.

"I was thinking we were going to lose more than our boots, you turkeys," Matt chided.

Soon all of them were singing the theme music to "Deliverance." They never saw the mountain men again that day; but they kept a watch out for them.

The rest of the day was spent hiking trails and basking in the beauty of unspoiled woods. That night the men stayed up longer than they had planned because they didn't want to admit it but they were keeping watch just in case the poachers came back.

Dan slept fitfully that night. The woods had a different feel to them from the day before. Then Dan was awakened by Peter speaking softly to Mark. Dan peered at his watch it was about three o'clock in the morning. Peter was telling Mark, he had awoken to an unintelligible cry far off in the woods. He listened from the cozy warmth of his sleeping bag, but he couldn't make it out. It sounded like someone yelling Hey, hey, hey, over and over again? Dan reluctantly crawled out of his warm sack and put on his jacket, and stepped out into the pitch black night. There was no moon and it was blackest night in the woods except for the stars way overhead, up past the trees and cliffs. The cry didn't sound like any animal he knew, rather a human yelling the same thing over and over.

Peter went deeper into the darkness away from the tents and yelled back, "Do you need help?" Silence!

And then he heard it clearly, "Help!" Someone was yelling help. It sounded far away, but in the gorge sound does funny things. Peter went back to the camp to awaken some others to form a

26

search party. Dan, Mark, George, and Matt were already getting dressed for the night air. They had also heard the sounds. Peter told them someone was in trouble and they were down the cliffs, pretty far away. Someone speculated that it might be a trap, but Peter put that notion down right away. They got several flashlights and started off in the direction of the voice. Keeping on the trail was the biggest challenge to the group of four. Once you got off the right path you were headed for trouble. The next hurdle was to keep from tripping over all the obstacles on the trail in the dark. The beams of the flashlights were their life saver. They followed the slivers of light in the black night. The voice got louder and clearer. After hiking over a half mile they became profoundly aware of how far they had gone from the camp. They stuck to the trail. It was clear the voice was calling, "help!" Peter yelled, "Who are you?"

The response came, "Help me."

Further into the depths of the gorge they traveled, following the cries for help, until one of them caught sight of a figure in the beam of his flashlight. They approached a boy who was crawling toward them. His face was all scratched up and contorted in pain. Mark bent over the figure on the ground. Mark asked him who he was. He said his name was Isaiah. He explained he had fallen off a cliff in the late afternoon, and had tried walking on his hurt leg back to the road, but the pain got so bad all he could do was crawl. When they asked him what he was doing in the woods, he told them that he was out hunting with his kin and they separated looking for game. Isaiah said his uncle was going to skin him alive because he had left his rifle when he couldn't carry it any more. They asked if his family was worried about him and if he thought they were they out looking for him. "Don't know for sure," Isaiah said, "since they's always in the woods for days on end."

Matt was a doctor and he examined the injured leg of Isaiah. He appeared to be about sixteen. The lower leg bone was broken. Matt was amazed he had gotten that far because the pain must be terrific. The kid said, "It kinda hurt real good."

They knew they had to carry him up hill for almost a mile in the dark. They knew they could not leave him. They took turns, two by two, carrying him up the steep trail. They had devised a seat out of their belts and suspended him between them. The doctor had fashioned a crude splint on his leg with branches and shoelaces. The kid never complained. It took over an hour and a half to climb back to the camp ground. When they got back everyone was awake and they immediately knew that this boy had to be taken to a hospital. They drove in Mark's old SUV because it had the biggest reclining back seat for the boy to ride in. When they left Red River Gorge State park, they went through the tiny town of Slade, and headed west onto the interstate for Lexington, Kentucky. They got the kid into the emergency room and they figured they had done their good deed when a nurse came out and said they had to complete some paper work. After not being able to answer most of the questions Mark and Dan went back to where they were working on the boy's leg to get his help answering the questions. When they got to the questions about insurance Isaiah said there was none. They wanted to know who would be responsible for his hospital expenses and the kid said nobody. This causes some distress to the intake nurse's composure. Matt, George, Dan, and Peter looked at each other. Mark said he would be responsible for the medical bills, and he signed the papers. With that resolved they left the hospital.

On the way back to the gorge Dan asked Mark if he knew what he was doing signing for the kid? Mark said he knew exactly what he was doing. Dan asked him, "Why did you agree to pay his hospital bills?"

"Because," Mark said, "that is what Jesus would do."

Chapter 4 - Lightning Strikes

The camping trip profoundly affected Dan's faith. He had acquired an appreciation for the mystery of the Creator and was astonished at the generosity of Mark for a stranger at the hospital. He found out later that Mark and Thad had kept in touch with the boy the rescued in the gorge and he had done well and was sent home after three days. In the following days and weeks Dan worked his job, studied the Bible, attended the men's group, and started praying regularly. Since no one had taught him how to pray he just talked to God about whatever was on his mind. Sometimes he wondered if that was OK, or if prayer should be more formal? He became intrigued with the prospect of attending a church but had many strong reservations about such a radical move.

He didn't want to be found out by all the holy people at church that he was a big time sinner. By his reckoning he had broken all the Ten Commandments consistently during his life. Some of the commandments he had only broken in thoughts and not deeds, but Jesus said it was just like doing it to think about doing it. He imagined he would be spotted right away in a church full of holy Joes. He also knew from experience that some so called religious people he had known were hypocrites. Why go to church with a bunch of hypocrites? The men he knew in the group he attended were genuine in their faith but they could be the exception. Another reservation he felt was an aversion to being a religious nut. It was working for him growing in his relationship with Jesus on a private and personal basis but he didn't want to be identified as a cult follower. Then there was the question of which church is the best church. Everybody was bias toward their own church and he didn't want to visit every church in the city shopping around. He prayed and prayed and didn't feel like he was being heard.

Hartwell United Methodist Church was where most of the support group attended and he decided that it would be the biggest risk to go there. What if he didn't like it? Then he would be uncomfortable in the men's group because he knew some of those men were very involved in that church. How could he maintain their friendship if he rejected their church? For every impulse he had to try church he came up with more objections to attend. There was a committee of voices in his head fighting him at every turn.

One evening at the men's group, Mark asked him if he would like to attend a special service at his church because they were having a really good bluegrass group visiting. This gave him just the excuse he was looking for to attend church. He always loved bluegrass music and often searched for it on the car radio. He owned a number of bluegrass Cd's, which were favorites of his. That morning he struggled with what to wear because he didn't know the dress code at the church. He decided, based on his experience as a child to put on his best three piece suit, white shirt, and conservative tie. He looked most respectable. H e was well disguised for church.

The greeter welcomed him and gave him a worship bulletin. Dan was anxious to have a seat and uncover what was in the papers he had been given. He started down the side aisle to be as inconspicuous as possible when Peter spotted him and came around from the other side of the church and invited him to sit with his family. To his horror they were sitting near the front and he had planned to sit near the back in case he needed to escape quickly. Now he was trapped up front, but how could he reject the companionship of a friend? Peter introduced him to his wife and children and sat Dan next to himself. Everyone had opened their bulletins so Dan did the same. There was the order of worship and he felt more at ease because he had in writing the program. Maybe this was going to be alright. The band started to assemble on the chancel and this looked like any other concert except for the stained glass windows and the big wooden cross hanging on the wall. The minister came out of a door in the front of the room and proceeded to greet and chat with people. Dan thought he looked like a politician running for office. When the minister came by the pew where Peter and his family were seated he was introduced to the minister. The minister replied he had looked forward to meeting him. That set off alarms in Dan because he suspected he was in a trap. But the minister moved on to the next pew without any more comments. Dan couldn't look at Peter because he wanted to ask him what he had said about him to the minister. Soon the musicians started playing a prelude and the minister scurried up front and sat in a high back chair behind a pulpit. The band opened with "Will the circle be Unbroken." They played three numbers for the prelude and then the minister came out and gave a greeting and introduced the band. The minister said a brief prayer and introduced the first hymn, "How Great thou Art."

When the congregation began to sing "How Great Thou Art" something broke inside Dan. In spite of all of his efforts tears started running down his face. This was most embarrassing and he wanted to hide. Thank God no one was paying any attention to him. Everyone was engrossed in praising God with this favorite hymn. Peter's wife Sue had handed him a hymnal opened to the right page so he could follow the words. It was difficult to sing and cry at the same time. He didn't understand where all these emotions were coming from. He was feeling an ecstasy he had never known and a overwhelming release of emotion beyond comprehension. He fleeting wondered if he was losing his mind. Later in the service he tried to distract himself from the waves of emotions he was having by looking at the stained glass windows. That was a bigger mistake. As the morning sun streamed into the sanctuary trough the brilliantly colored glass shafts of light were shining on the heads of different people. Instead of ordinary people they were transformed into visions of otherworldly beauty in the beams of colored light. Dan had to look away because he was seeing people in a light that made him feel a love for them that was like the love Jesus had made him feel that day in the woods.

The pastor read several passages from the Bible and preached on Psalm 139. This begins, "O Lord you have searched me and known me." Every word of that psalm rocked Dan's world and he was totally absorbing every word the pastor spoke. When the pastor concluded the sermon with the last lines of the psalm Dan was convicted of the truth it contained. "Search me, me O God and know my heart; test me and know my thoughts. See if there is any wicked way in me, and lead me in the way everlasting." Dan was totally yes to God. He was getting his composure and things were settling down in his heart. The offering was accompanied by more of the band and his spirits lightened when they played "Foggy Mountain Breakdown." But God was not going to let him off quite that easily that morning. The closing hymn was "Blessed Assurance." The congregation loved this hymn although they rarely sung it anymore. The chorus is, "This is my story, this is my song. Praising my savior all the day long." Dan never wanted it to end, but it did. Peter didn't ask him if he enjoyed the service because he was perfectly aware that his friend was ecstatic.

After the service there was fellowship in the huge basement of the church. Dan was led downstairs to the Fellowship hall and introduced to too many people. He was impressed with how ordinary these people actually were. In the worship he had seen them as a heavenly choir bathed in Divine light. Down stairs they were the exact same people you meet at the supermarket. Young , old, tall, short, heavy , thin, and everything in between. There were several disabled people who were particularly popular it seemed. This was quite a mix of humanity. There was no way to distinguish the saints from the sinners. He was trying to analyze the visible church and completely oblivious to the invisible church, which would only become more known in time. A couple of people invited him to different activities such as Adult Sunday School classes and mission project. He politely declined all invitations. He was overwhelmed by the worship. Some bold old man asked him if he was a first timer visitor. Dan replied, "Yes."

The man said, "Well lighting didn't strike ya, did it?" He said the same thing to every new face he saw.

Dan said, "Guess not." But the truth and Dan knew it that lightning had struck him. He was going back to church next Sunday and whenever he could from that time on. Something about being in a group of people worshipping God was more intense than being by oneself. The pastor made a special point of saying goodbye to him when he left the Fellowship Hall.

Chapter 5 - The Visit

The business of making a living kept Dan in constant motion. He had invested his life in his company and he was not about to jeopardize that investment of a lifetime by too many distractions. When the pastor from the church called and asked if he could visit, Dan was reluctant because he preferred remaining noncommittal concerning his participation in the church. There was a freedom in being a spectator to the drama of the church. It was easier to enjoy the benefits without being involved in the mess of human interactions in a church. He had other reservations about getting to close to the church. There was no comfortable way to reject the pastor's request so he made a date for the visit.

Dan tidied up the house so he would make a favorable impression on his guest. Since the only occupants of the house where he and Mindy they lived as they pleased. The furnishings were sparse as Dan was acquiring things slowly. It had a certain Spartan look in its simplicity. He had purchased some mission style pieces from an Amish store in West Liberty, Ohio. This furniture was solid oak and there was no particle board or veneers. The craftsmanship was immaculate and built to last forever. Dan loved quality and had the resources to pay for it. Mindy appreciated the comfort of the furniture as well. Mindy slept on the leather cushioned chairs whenever Dan was gone.

When Pastor Andy arrived he was greeted with the typical rudeness of a dog. This is just dog's familiarity. Pastor Andy seemed oblivious to the invasion of his personal space as he was probed by the inquisitive Mindy. Dan apologized for the poor manners and explained they had few visitors recently. That was the truth since he had become reclusive in his home life. Dan invited Pastor Andy to sit in one of the two mission recliners in the living room. He asked him if he wanted something to drink. The pastor declined the offer but thanked him for offering. Dan was beginning to regret having the pastor come into his home because it felt awkward. Fortunately the pastor was experienced at putting people at ease and took the initiative in starting the conversation.

"Dan you have been attending worship frequently at our church, and I have been hoping to get to know you," said Pastor Andy. "There is no opportunity to have a extended conversation with someone right after church because everyone wants to talk church business. Frankly it is hard to keep straight all the information thrown at me by dozens of people. Many of the people have contact with me on Sunday morning and that's it. So tell me about yourself and what brought you to our church?"

Dan was not really prepared to give his life story over to a relative stranger so he blurted out a summary of some facts. He told about his educational background. He briefly mentioned he was going through a divorce. He reluctantly stated he was not much of a churchgoer, which was a colossal understatement. Then he remembered the second question and said he had known Peter for a long time and had been attending the men's support group and had come to know some of the men in that group. Those were the reasons he was visiting Hartwell Church. Of course he excluded his spiritual experiences because he didn't want to appear crazy to the pastor by revealing his spiritual experiences.

Pastor Andy sensed Dan had been truthful but evasive in his response, so he decided to try another tack. "You know I was not always a pastor. Actually before I became involved in the church I was a teacher in Indiana at a High School. There was a period in my life when I had nothing to do with religion. I went to Purdue as a premed major determined to be a doctor. After failing biochemistry twice I settled on teaching science as a more realistic career. It was after fifteen years of teaching that I got the call back to the church. Raising kids in our society, made my wife and I decide they needed some moral foundation. That is how God drew us into the church. Pretty soon I was leading the youth group, and I was winging it, just trying to stay one step ahead of the kids' questions about what we believed. Thank God they didn't know how little I understood. But you know us teachers, 'just give me the book and we can teach it?' Well the more I learned, the more I wanted to know. I started taking a few classes at a seminary to better understand the Christian faith. It was around that time that I asked Jesus into my life, and here I am pasturing a church. That's where I am coming from."

Dan was surprised by the openness of the pastor and how matter of fact was his testimony. He imagined this was the Reader's Digest version. But it was not very spectacular. It did appear credible. Dan took a chance and opened up with a bit more with his history. "My stepping into the church began the day I was determined to blow my brains out. Other than this dog I saw no reason to live any longer. When I was about to pull the trigger I called out to Jesus and he came to me and stopped me. Because he was there for me I have been trying to understand this faith thing ever since. Probably most people would say I'm crazy, but I know what happened. He gave me a new life. He changed me in ways it is hard to describe. I wouldn't believe it, except it happened to me. I don't want to be a religious nut case. Maybe I am one and just can't admit it. Anyways why do I need to go to church when Jesus and I are tight? No offense, but why should I be part of a religion? Isn't God just as real here with me and my dog as He is in church?"

Pastor Andy lived for these moments. This is why he went into the ministry to deal with these questions. So he replied, "You are not crazy. People have been experiencing the risen Christ for two thousand years and you are in good company. The risen Christ is the reason why there is a Christian church. You are also absolutely right about God. God is as present here as he is at the church, or everywhere for that matter. Church is a group of people called by the Holy Spirit to encourage one another to grow in the Christian faith, and to worship God. God doesn't need us but we need God. We come to God in our brokenness, in our sinfulness, in our need for forgiveness, and desire to be loved. That is where we are healed and God gives us grace. We give praise to God in prayer, song, listening to the word of God, and in the interpretation of the word. The church spreads the gospel in word and in the act of mission. Ok, you got me going, but I do love the church. The church is the Body of Christ. That is why I am in love with the church. In spite of all the flaws and human frailties, it is the Body of Christ. The church is where we meet Jesus"

"That was some rant. I mean it was good. I get the part about worship. I thought we were trying to buy God's favor. That made no sense to me because what does God need from us? God is God, so what can we give that God needs? Aren't people praising God to get something out of the deal?"

"Some people may think that, but that is not Christian worship. We give God glory because God is worthy. True worship is a full spirit contact sport. We come into the presence to love God in thought, word, and deed. It is not a spectator sport and it is not entertainment. It is the work of the Body of Christ to adore God. Worship is about giving to God, not getting something from God. Do you know the commandment to love God with all your heart, mind, and soul? That is perfectly expressed in worship. And the other work of the church is the mission and evangelism which are inseparable. We are the hands, and feet of Christ in the world. That work of the church goes on seven days a week twenty-four hours a day all over the world."

"Are you serious?"

"Totally serious! There is ministry and evangelism taking place in hundreds of settings on every continent at this minute and our church is a part of some of that ministry through financial support and in many situations by active participation. There are people engaged in mission in this city, state, nation, and around the world working for the Body of Christ. I really want to encourage you to learn more about what the church does. We will be having an inquiring class for people interested in the church starting in a couple of weeks and it would be an honor if you would consider being a part of the class. I believe you will find it very informative."

They talked about the time and place of the class. Dan replied that he would seriously consider it. What concerned him was being stuck in a class with a group of strangers at his age. It sounded too much like going back to Sunday school. The fact that he was profoundly ignorant of what he church did, it gave him a compelling reason to try the class. Since the pastor was teaching the class it should make it interesting. The pastor was not particularly impressive in appearance, but he was knowledgeable, and seemed genuine in his faith in Jesus.

Again Dan offered the pastor something to drink. Pastor Andy accepted the offer. When Dan suggested a beer there was a moment of indecision in the response from the pastor. He apologized and asked for a coke instead because he had a meeting to attend and beer would make him drowsy. They had cokes together and Dan asked him if he liked hunting. The pastor shared that he enjoyed hunting but had not had any opportunities in the past few years. Dan took him to the basement, unlocked his gun cabinet, and showed him his hunting rifles. When Dan unlocked the strongbox where he kept his collection of Civil War pistols he recoiled in shock. The pistols were gone. Dan hadn't looked at his valuable collection of rare pistols in many months but this is where they were stored. How could they be gone? He was visibly upset. The pastor assured him there had to be an explanation. Dan confided to the pastor they were worth tens of thousands of dollars. This was the right time for the pastor to leave.

Dan searched the house top to bottom but there was no sign of his collection of pistols.

Chapter 6 - All You Need Is Love

Dan had hoped he would magically become a saint the day he met Jesus. Dan struggled with his human frailties every day. Some days it was positively discouraging how little he was able to control his thoughts. His words and deeds were mostly undergoing a radical transformation that caused him serious estrangement with his older acquaintances. The most guilt he felt was over unholy thoughts when he was praying, and when he was at church. Sometimes it was almost comical how his mind would stray into the land of lust without his conscious intention he was traveling down that road. He wondered if he was the only one plagued with sexual desires. He had no idea how others dealt with this dilemma because he was too ashamed to bring it up among his Christian friends.

During worship he found himself positioning himself a few rows behind an attractive women in her forties who attended church with her son and daughter. He did notice she wore a wedding ring so he never even tried to speak with her. Since his own divorce was going so slowly, he had not dated and was craving the company of a woman. He was disgusted with himself that he was feeling such a need, and it was becoming focused on this woman who had never done anything to encourage him, except to radiate her beauty in church. He was convinced she must intuitively sense his attention. He was starting to obsess over her during the week and was anxious for Sunday to arrive so he could see her again. After weeks of this infatuation he summoned all of his courage and asked Peter if he knew her. Peter knew her very well because they had mutual friends and had spent time together at parties before she separated from her husband. The breakup of the marriage had taken place a couple of years ago and they had only a passing acquaintance since. This information was what Dan wanted to hear. She might be available for a date if she had not already found someone. Peter had informed him that her name was Susan Hopkins and her children were Troy and Dianna.

When you haven't dated in decades and you want to ask someone out, how do you go about it? That question haunted Dan. There was no way he was going to approach her and introduce himself. That was too bold and risked rejection at the start. This was not high school where you could ask a friend to ask the person if they liked you. Dan was stymied by how to get an introduction. Thankfully Peter finally figured out why Dan was asking about Susan and had found out that Susan was not seeing anyone. After worship one Sunday during the fellowship time in the basement Peter maneuvered Dan close to Susan and introduced them. The eye contact between Dan and Susan was intense. There was a mutual interest. Susan had noticed the attention he had been giving her and her instincts were immediately confirmed by the way he stared into her eyes. The conversation went to Susan's teenage daughter Dianna. Susan told Dan about her daughter's figure skating and that they were leaving church soon to go home and get ready for a figure skating competition that afternoon. Troy was off to a friend's house for the afternoon. Dan said he would love to see her skate and asked if she would mind if he came by to watch. Susan kindly replied she would enjoy the company. The conversation ended when glanced at her watch, excused herself, gathered Troy and Dianna, and was out the door.

Dan could not remember feeling as giddy as he felt as she left the room. He wanted to make an announcement to the whole room she had said yes. Of course he controlled himself, but it was difficult to not jump around the fellowship hall. If anyone bothered to pay close attention to him, they would have noticed he was beaming.

Back at Dan's home he rummaged through his clothes looking for appropriate ice skating rink fashion. The sweater he chose smelled of mothballs. He found some heavy socks because he knew his feet would get cold at the rink. When he passed through the dining room he stopped at the piles of papers on the table. Laid out before him was the documentation of his life as he prepared to meet with the attorneys and his wife at the mediator's office to work out the financial settlement agreement for the divorce. Tax forms, bank statements, investments, real estate documents, and the financial accounts from his business and bank were stacked in neat piles. He pondered the importance of these documents and doubted the meaning of it all. "Is this the sum total of my life," Dan wondered? "Does any of this validate who I really am? When I am gone all of this ends up in the dump. What's the point of this? Who cares? If there is ever going to be something between me and Susan I need to clean up this mess before we get in too deep. Is this going to make God mad? Does God care? Watching a teenager figure skater isn't exactly bigamy. This is innocent enough." Dan tore himself away from these thoughts of the debris of his divorce, and drove to the ice rink.

Susan's cheeks were rosy as she stood up and waved to Dan as his eyes searched the stands for her among the small crowd of parents and siblings watching the completion. Susan looked adorable bundled up in winter clothes in the chilly atmosphere of the ice rink. They kept a proper distance between each other on the hard stands as they watched the skaters. After some small talk, Dan told her he needed to tell her something important about himself. He outlined the history of his marriage and precisely where they were in the divorce proceeding. He knew it was not right to expect anything of Susan considering he was technically still married, but he was hoping for friendship more than anything else. That was the truth. He didn't miss the pain of a hostile relationship: what he missed was the joy of a female companion. He did have desires for Susan and he did have fantasies of them making love, but even more than those things, he wanted a female friend. As he sat next to Susan and the fragrance of her perfume drifted toward him he realized how much he missed his wife. What he missed was the joy of a female companion. He didn't miss the pain of a hostile relationship.

Susan was an elementary school teacher and she was confident, strong, and very gentle. She had long brown hair, brown eyes, and a beautiful figure. Dan guessed she was about five foot eight inches tall. He could easily imagine her beautiful body. She dressed modestly but it did not hide her form. Dan wanted to hold her hand but that would be way to bold a move at this stage in the relationship. He offered to get her some coffee or hot chocolate. She was touched by the gesture since it had been many years before; someone had done something for her. She had always been waiting on her ex-husband and children. While she was attracted to Dan, she was only interested in friendship. She was not going to get involved with a married man, divorce pending or not.

When Dan came back with the hot chocolates, she told him a little about herself. She had been teaching for over twenty years. She had wanted more children, but there were problems in the marriage and she had waited before they had more children to resolve the problems. Eventually she knew she was in an impossible situation and she left her ex-husband and took her children with her. Her ex had restricted visitation with Troy and Dianna and they rarely spoke. She had dated a few men, but she didn't want the involvement they were looking for in a relationship. She missed having another adult to talk with and hoped she and Dan might become friends.

These boundaries she had laid out worked for Dan. He told her that this was all he was looking for as well. The fact was they were already falling in love and neither of them was about to admit it to themselves or anyone else.

Suddenly Diana came on the ice in her magical pale blue and gold skater's outfit. She looked like an angel. She skated to one of Chopin's Etudes and she performed her routine without a flaw. Dan admired her athletic ability and poise. Watching a magnificent fourteen year old glide over the ice to Chopin was really special. He stole glances at Susan's face who intently followed her daughter's every move on the ice. The leaps and bounds were awesome. Dan was so glad he had come.

Susan most admired her daughter's confidence overcoming obstacles that had been devastating to youthful development. Susan wasn't going to confide to Dan the dark secrets of her past life. The fewer people knew the better. Watching a magnificent fourteen year old glide over the ice to Chopin was really special. He stole glances at Susan's face and intently following her daughter's every move on the ice. The leaps and bounds were awesome. Dan was so glad he had come.

When the competition was finished they were ecstatic that Dianna had won first place in her age group. Dan asked Susan, "could we go somewhere out to dinner to celebrate?" Susan declined the offer, explaining Dianna had homework to do, they had to pick up Troy from his friend's house, and Susan had preparation for her classes the next day. Susan hesitated and added, "Maybe another time." Although the invitation had been spontaneous, it was a huge disappointment to Dan. It must have showed on his face. Then when she relented a bit he was elated. These rapid emotional swings he was experiencing were making Dan nervous.

On the drive home Dan tried to recall the fragrance of Susan. He had caught the scent of her hair and it reminded him of exotic fruits. He loved her closeness and involvement with Dianna. She was so sweet and easy to be with. He wondered what had happened to her marriage. What sort of person was her ex husband? How did she manage on a teacher's salary? He knew he made ten times what she made in a year and it was not easy to get by on a fraction of what he had. He knew they were committed to a dinner date. Now it was just a matter of working out the details. He also knew in his heart she was going to be more than a friend.

Chapter 7 - Back to School

Wednesday night inquiring classes at the Hartwell United Methodist Church are taught by the Pastor Andy. He was enthusiastic about this group of potential new members because of the interesting mix of people. The ages ranged from early twenties to mid eighties, and the educational background was from High School drop out to postgraduate education. This diverse class was a challenge for Pastor Andy to communicate the essentials of the Christian faith and keeping everyone's attention. He was going to use a shotgun approach and pray he would hit heads and hearts as the Holy Spirit directed the faith.

The class began with each person introducing themselves with a description of their church background. Only one of the nine members of the class had ever belonged to a Methodist church. In the ever increasing mobility of American society people moved frequently and rarely had strong denominational loyalty. Americans are consumers and shop for churches just as they shop for goods to possess. Every church has its own character and Hartwell was a community that emphasized participation in mission and evangelism to the community and the world.

There were regular attendees at Hartwell who never joined the church, but most of the people made the commitment to be a member and support the church. Like most older long-established churches there was a core of long-time members who gave the majority of the financial support and were always dedicated to working at the activities of the church. The church was blessed by these faithful members who did not try to dominate the church and were genuinely excited to welcome and assimilate new people into its life. Pastor Andy could rely upon certain individuals to carry the load and keeping the work of the church going. The people in the class were oblivious to the politics of the church, but time would teach them the players and powers behind the scenes. Pastor Andy was also learning how the Holy Spirit was building the invisible church. Even among the active membership of Hartwell there were only a few who were aware of what the Spirit was doing.

Everyone in the class was given a copy of the Apostle's Creed. After a brief explanation of the history and significance of the Creed there was a line –by-line discussion of its meaning. This led into a lively discussion of the mystery of the Trinitarian understanding of One God, and that led into a even more animated look at the mystery of the Incarnation in the person of Jesus. The pastor took this as an opportunity to ask each person when they had come to know Jesus as the Son of God. Dan was amazed at the variety of ways people had come to a relationship with Jesus. Some had learned about Jesus in Sunday School classes, and they had grown in time to know about Him and to believe in Him as their Savior. Others had called upon Him during a crisis and had experienced a dramatic healing. One woman in her eighties testified she had always believed in Jesus and He was always with her. Dan was the newest believer in the room and he was in awe of the testimony of the others who had known Jesus so long. The person had fascinated him the most was the old woman who said she had always known Jesus. After class Dan approached the woman and asked, "How have you known Jesus all your life?"

She gave him a shy smile and replied, "He has always been right with me. That's all I know."

"That's incredible, Dan said, I mean I believe you but.... Have you ever been afraid?"

"No! Jesus is there for me, she said, and I know he's takin' care of me."

Dan was almost unable to respond, "Well I admire you. I mean that is so beautiful. I envy you. I wish I had what you've got."

"Listen here, she said, I'm nobody. I never graduated from High School. I'm just a housewife who raised her kids. You're an educated man, and you look like you got money. Why would you envy me?"

"You've always known Jesus, and you feel Him with you. That's what I want." The woman looked him in the eyes and smiled. The strangest change took place in her eyes. It was as if they became the eyes of Jesus looking at him. He wanted to hug her, but he was concerned she would not understand his intentions. He was gazing into the eyes of his Savior who occupied that sweet old face.

As Dan was driving home he was hardly aware of the SUV that was tailgating him. When he turned onto the entrance ramp of the freeway the SUV roared around him, forcing him onto the soft shoulder of the road. He barely avoided sinking his right tires into the soft shoulder and tumbling over into the grassy slope below. The adrenaline was pumping through him as he reflected on what might have happened. The taillights of the SUV disappeared into the stream of traffic on the freeway. That was too close.

Dan had no idea what that nearly catastrophic collision was about. The thought came to his mind there was something against him. He felt that attack was not a coincidence. Then another thought occurred to him stronger than the question about why something was after him. He was certain that he had been protected from the attack. He knew his wheel had gone off the pavement and he should be in the ditch. Instead he had mysteriously stayed upright and recovered.

It is probably for the best he was unaware what that attack was about because there were powers and principalities conspiring against him. His supernatural protectors had kept his car from sinking into the muck and flipping his car down the hill. When Dan thanked God for helping him avoid the accident he didn't know how the angels had intervened.

Meanwhile, the driver who almost ran him off the road never gave another thought to the compulsion he was under to race past the car ahead of him on the narrow one lane entrance ramp. That driver was so consumed with rage he only wanted to get past the car that was driving the speed limit and he was in a big hurry to get going. Anger clouded his mind and he was unwittingly a willing instrument to take a new follower of Jesus down.

Unbeknownst to Dan there was a battle taking place over his conversion to Christianity. He was in mortal danger, and the forces against him were escalating the warfare because Dan was moving close to becoming a member of the church which was considered the enemy. The adversary of God had been fighting God from the beginning of human history and there were times of great success, and other times of failure. Our present time was going well for those who opposed God. The Christian church in Europe and America was in steady decline and every form of greed and hedonism was raised up to emulate in the popular culture. Religion had been perverted by a few to make it appear ridiculous to the majority of people. The church was originally attacked with overt persecution by the Roman Empire. That had led to a systematic killing of the leaders and saints of the church for a few hundred years. But rather than driving people away, this persecution had the opposite effect of drawing more souls to the Body of Christ. Different strategies of attack had been tried and had failed. This newest form of warfare appeared to be successful: undermine the church and the Christian faith would eventually vanish from the face of the earth.

Dan knew nothing about his role in this ancient drama. He was oblivious to the importance he was to play in God's good purpose for those who love God. There is a design and it would be completed with the obedience of those who responded to the call to be part of the plan. Dan was never to be famous or even recognized by the world as anyone important. That is not what matters in the bigger picture. In God's plan Dan had the future responsibility of becoming a servant of the Lord Jesus Christ. That is the highest calling any human could ever know. The evil one knew this and was determined to stop it as soon as possible. God knows the past, the present, and the future, and knows every variation and possibility in the plan for every individual. In this vast knowing God has given the human creature the God-like gift of free will so that the individual chooses his or her own course. Something as seeming inconsequential as joining a church has eternal consequences. Dan could and would make many mistakes in this journey. What was important, however, he had replaced the core of his being from self importance to love and obedience to God's will in his relationship with Jesus. As a servant of God he had work to do in the great plan of salvation of souls.

When Dan got home he prayed and thanked God for Pastor Andy and the rest of the people at church. Then Dan was filled with emotion as he thanked God for that old woman and her plain testimony. He asked God to give him the faith she had. Dan asked for this good gift. That is a prayer that cannot be refused. The angels danced.

Chapter 8 - Soup and Sandwiches

As the months went by Dan found his life becoming very routine. Susan had become an important part of his life. They were both determined to take it slow because they were cautious about getting hurt. Dan was frequently traveling for his business. He had completed the inquirers' class at the church and had joined the church. He tried to never miss Sunday worship. By attending worship he felt part of something bigger than himself. Worship was becoming an important part of his rebuilding himself. Life was good and getting better. Dan was thanking God in his prayers which had become a regular part of his life. He prayed when he awoke, he prayed when he went to bed at night, he prayed when he showered, he prayed when he ate, and anytime he had an impulse to pray. On his trips to developing countries he prayed more than usual because of the poverty that was impossible to ignore. What disturbed him the most was children begging for food. That was so troublesome because he didn't know what to do about it. He prayed God would show him a way to do something about hunger.

During worship it was common for a member of the congregation to give a brief testimony about one of the missions they were involved in through the church. On this particular Sunday God gave Dan an opportunity to have his prayer answered. A young woman Dan did not recognize stood in front and talked about a soup kitchen she had worked at the day before. She was overcome with emotion talking about the several hundred people they served and their gratitude for the simple meal of soup and sandwiches. As she concluded her emotional description of the experience, she extended an invitation to anyone present to come the next Saturday to the inner-city soup kitchen and help prepare and serve the food to the hungry. After the service was over Dan looked for the young woman with the compelling testimony. He had a hard time locating her and only found her as she was leaving the church. He introduced himself and told her that he would like to go with her on Saturday to help out. She told him the address of the downtown church and that he needed to show up at eight-thirty.

The church Dan was looking for was in a run-down part of town with which he was not familiar, and he mistook the steeple of an old Catholic church for the one he wanted. He was uncomfortable parking his Lexus in this neighborhood. This area was once the heart of the slaughterhouse industry of the city. Now there were only a few businesses still operating. Most of the factory buildings were abandoned with broken windows and boarded up doors. The residents were primarily from Appalachia. This part of town was alive with drug pushers, prostitution, and the poorest of the poor. Dan noticed he was being carefully observed by the young men on the street corners. Hopefully parking in front of the church building would be his insurance against anything happening. The front doors were locked, so he made his way around to the back of the buildingwhere he found an unlocked door. Once inside, the smells of food and cigarettes filled his nostrils. The lights were on in the kitchen which was close to the backdoor. The sanctuary was on the second floor and offices, classrooms, social hall, and kitchen on the ground floor. The kitchen was equipped like a restaurant, and there was a man muttering to himself working over a meat-slicer. Dan said in a hesitant tone, "Hello. I'm here to help with the soup kitchen."

The older, short, rotund man looked him over and said, "Go wash your hands. And there's an apron in the hall you can use."

Dan found the aprons hanging on hooks and put one on. He returned to the kitchen. He introduced himself to the elderly man who was concentrating on feeding a large loaf of luncheon meat into the electric slicer. He just glanced back at Dan and replied, "I'm Reverend Bob. Do you know how to work a meat-slicer?"

"I think I can handle it." Dan replied.

"Good you can slice up those loaves of lunch meat while I start the soup," Reverend Bob responded.

Reverend Bob lit three burners on the stove, half filled three four gallon pots with hot water, put them on the ten burner gas stove, and started dumping ingredients into the pots. It became evident that he was making chicken noodle soup.

Dan was keenly aware of the danger involved in using the meat slicer. One slip and he would be sliced by the razor-sharp spinning blade. As soon as he sliced one ten pound loaf of meat he stacked it on a tray. He then stripped the casing off the next loaf and started slicing. After finishing off the six loaves of meat he asked what he should do next.

"Go back in the pantry and get the bread," Reverend Bob said, "and you can start making the sandwiches."

There were cartons of sliced white bread stacked up in the pantry, along with boxes of pastries and some cakes and pies. This was clearly "day old" returned bakery products. All the bakery products were damaged in some fashion. Dan hauled two cartons of bread back into the kitchen and set them on the counter. Then Reverend Bob instructed him on how to put two slices of luncheon meat on a slice of bread, spread a dab of yellow mustard on the meat, cover it with a slice of bread, and stack the finished sandwich in a huge plastic box. He was told to make four hundred sandwiches. He was also informed to work fast because they didn't have much time, they needed to load the church van by eleven thirty. As they were working, Dan asked if anybody else was coming to help. Reverend Bob shook his head, "In this business you never know," he said. "But it's early in the month."

Dan worked as fast as he could, but soon realized there was a limit as to how fast he could make a sandwich and keep it reasonably neat. While he was working a woman who appeared to be in her eighties in a faded print dress showed up, made herself a cup of coffee, and helped herself to one of the donuts from the partially crushed boxes of donuts from the pantry. She walked around like this was her kitchen, and she sampled the soup on the stove.

"Too much pepper." She said in disgust to Reverend Bob. "Why do you put so much pepper in the soup?"

"I know what my customers like, and who asked you anyways?" Reverend Bob asked, "Beulah get home from the hospital yesterday?" There proceeded to be a long conversation between Reverend Bob and the woman whose name was Lillie Mae about the health and affairs of numerous people. Some of the subjects were just out of jail while others were facing the prospect of going to jail. They ignored Dan altogether.

When the sandwiches were completed and two big containers were filled, Dan asked what was next to do. Reverend Bob had him load the van parked by the backdoor with the partially crushed boxes of bakery products. Then he was instructed on how to make a watery drink mix in five gallon plastic thermos containers. The containers reminded Dan of the orange and white water container he remembered seeing at construction sites. Dan made two of them. Dan could barely lift them once they were filled. By the time they loaded everything into the van it was almost eleven thirty. The floor of the van was filled with all the food, drink mix, and paper products. "You can ride with me," Reverend Bob said to Dan.

Dan had assumed he was only going to help make the food and had not anticipated serving. He had no idea where they were going and was too proud to ask so he sat in the van next to Lillie Mae and just kept quiet. As they bounced along the potholed streets of the inner city Reverend Bob turned to him and said, "Remember you are serving Jesus!"

When they arrived outside an old decrepit storefront, there was a long line of people waiting. Dan estimated there were over a hundred people standing there. Reverend Bob parked the van in the alley towards the back of the building by the side door. Several men were waiting for the van and immediately came over, opened the doors of the van, and started carrying the food into the building. Reverend Bob introduced Dan to a man named Kojak who was the boss of the soup kitchen. When Dan shook Kojak's hand he was impressed with his strong and rock hard grip. Kojak was definitely not someone to mess with. Kojak told Dan he would be serving the soup. So Dan carried one of the big pots of hot soup to the front room which was the serving and eating area. As he crossed the threshold into the room he caught his heel on the raised threshold, stumbled, and splashed about a quart of the soup out of the pot. The steaming hot liquid soaked the front of his khaki pants. Someone grabbed a rag and wiped the mess off the floor. Not much to do about the big wet stain on the front of Dan's pants. Of course it was embarrassing since it looked like he wet himself. It was time to let the hungry people in. Soon everyone who could fit into the room were lined up from the door to the serving area, Kojak called for a prayer. Everyone bowed their heads and Kojak prayed in a loud voice. He asked God to bless the food and to bless the people. He closed the prayer with the words, "In the blessed name of our Savior Jesus Christ," and a great "Amen!" came from the gathered people. Dan had never heard such an enthusiastic and loud "amen" in his church.

The line moved very quickly, and soon all those who had been waiting on the sidewalk were served. More people kept appearing at the door and entering the soup kitchen. A family of five came into the crowded room and Kojak rushed over and blocked their entry. A loud fight began between Kojak and the father. Kojak was insistent that they leave and was trying to move the family out the door. They were on the verge of a fist fight. Reverend Bob rushed over, interjected himself between the two angry men. The two men went silent and dropped their fists. Kojak turned in disgust and went into the back room. The family of five came forward for their lunch. "What was that all about?" Dan asked Reverend Bob.

"Kojak knows that family," He answered. "The father and mother spend all their welfare money and food stamps on dope. That's why they bring the children to the soup kitchen, because they don't have any money left for food. Kojak just can't stand people that don't take care of their children. Good thing they backed off because Kojak used to be a professional boxer. He would have laid that guy out with one punch."

Dan was sympathetic to Kojak's indignation, but also believed that children shouldn't suffer because of the sickness of the parents.

Dan was emotionally overloaded after interacting with the almost two hundred people he had just served. With a few exceptions the people sincerely expressed their gratitude for the meager meal. The beauty of the faces looking into his eyes as he handed them a sandwich was overwhelming. They came in every age, shape, and form, those who were very well dressed to homeless families. Dan thought to himself every one of them had a story which he didn't know and he wondered what had brought them to a soup kitchen. Reverend Bob knew most of the people and spent his time in conversation with many of them. Dan was hoping there might be some food left over to satisfy his own hunger. He was starving since he hadn't eaten all day. Finally he couldn't stand it anymore and he grabbed a sandwich and wolfed it down. He was amazed how good that lunch meat sandwich tasted, with a dash of yellow mustard, on that old white bread. The pastries they had brought were all out on a table for people to take with them. They disappeared pretty fast. After every one was fed, Kojak yelled second helpings were ready and most people came through the line again. Then the food was gone.

Around one o'clock they gathered up all the pots and containers and loaded them back into the van. Back at the church building they unloaded the empty containers and began washing everything. Dan discovered how truly sharp the edge of the circular blade of the meat slicer was when he was wiping it clean. He removed a hunk of skin off his knuckle before he felt the pain. Lillie Mae immediately got the first aid box and wrapped it in gauze and bandaged his finger. This is when Lillie Mae started bossing Dan and Reverend Bob. She took over the clean-up of the kitchen and made sure everything was spotless. When they had thoroughly cleaned the kitchen and washed the floor, Reverend Bob invited Dan to lunch at the local chili parlor. Dan was surprised by this sudden display of interest in him since he felt indifference all morning.

The chili parlor was mostly empty at two o'clock in the afternoon. Reverend Bob opened up and shared some of his life story with Dan. But mostly he was artfully trying to find out what motivated Dan to come to the soup kitchen. Dan was sensed that he had passed the initial test and was being interviewed for future responsibilities. He really liked Reverend Bob who was very salty and down to earth. Reverend Bob seemed incapable of asking for help, even though he was in desperate need with all of his various ministries in this inner-city mission church. Dan was intrigued with this unassuming man who was living the gospel of Jesus Christ. He didn't know such people existed except as well known saints like Mother Theresa. Of course

Reverend Bob would have been offended if anyone even suggested he was saintly. To make certain no one accused him of being a saintly person; he would resort to his assortment of ribald jokes, which he told with great flourish. A bond was developing between these two men.

Dan was excited about being a part of the church that is almost invisible to the world. Dan was unaware these ministries to the poor that happen all over the world and involve thousands of missionaries striving to obey the commandments of Jesus Christ continue unnoticed by the news media, the government, or the general public. Like Reverend Bob, they survive on marginal salaries, struggle to meet the needs of the people they serve, receive little encouragement, and are frequently met with criticism even from their fellow Christians. Dan was picking up on this over his luncheon conversation with Reverend Bob. Dan became increasingly aware of this crushing burden as their relationship grew.

Later Dan called Susan to tell her about his amazing discovery and hoped she would join him next Saturday in feeding the multitude. Dan was also thinking about who else he could recruit.

Chapter 9 - Charity

Susan invited Dan over when he called after working at the soup kitchen. He sounded so excited over the phone and he wanted to talk to her. When she opened the door he hugged her before he was inside the house. She wondered if he was ever going to let her go as he enveloped her in his arms. Finally he released her just enough to kiss her on the lips. Then he stopped and let her step back to catch her breath. What had aroused him so much at the soup kitchen, she wondered. He was breathing faster than usual and couldn't wait to tell her of the day's events. They sat on the sofa and he looked in her eyes as he began his tale.

"It was not what I expected," he began. "Well, it was just what you might imagine a soup kitchen would be, except it's different than what you think it is. The people are like you and me. Some are different, but they are really no different. Does that make any sense? You know I could be on the other side of the table asking for food. I could see myself standing in that line waiting with all those people and holding out my hand for the soup and sandwich. I know that it's only something that put me on the side of the table giving food and something that put them on the other side of the serving table. Like maybe they are disabled, or out of work, or have a prison record and can't find a job, or they could be mentally screwed up and just don't function, or they are uneducated, or whatever. They are not bad people. They're just people. And they're no different than you and me. Something weird happened when we were driving to the soup kitchen. Reverend Bob said they were the Christ or something like that. That haunted me the whole time I was dishing out the soup. Was I serving Jesus? What did he mean, 'they are the Christ?'"

"In Matthew's Gospel," Susan interjected, "Jesus said, 'I was hungry and you gave me food. I was thirsty and you gave me something to drink. Just as you did it to one of the least of these you did it to me.' I think that is what he meant. Do you think so?"

Dan thought for a minute and said, "Amazing! You got it. I wish I knew the Bible like you do. That's it. There is this supernatural thing going on and I felt it in my heart, but I didn't know it in my head. That's it! I was serving Jesus." Dan stopped as tears began flowing from his eyes. Susan embraced him and held him for a while. "Susan I really want you to come with me next Saturday and maybe we could bring Dianna. She would love it. The pastor who makes the food is a character. I think you are going to really like him. He needs help. He really needs help. I'm going to call him this week and I'll see what I can do to help him. These people need vegetables and we didn't give them any. There is so much we could do. You should hear these people pray. It's not what they pray, but how they pray. They say it like they mean it. I could feel their faith. Do you know what I mean?"

"Dan, I've been to some inner-city churches," she replied, "and they are filled with the Holy Spirit and are not ashamed to show it. My former husband Jay started taking us to a downtown church for awhile. He said our church was dead and he wanted a Spirit filled church. Dianna, Troy, and I have been there and done that."

"What happened? Why did you stop going there if it was so good?"

"Jay decided the preacher talked too much about tithing and he didn't like that. So we went to another church on the other side of the city. And after awhile he found something wrong with that church. After several more churches Dianna, Troy, and I went back to Hartwell and Dan eventually found the 'Lighthouse Fellowship of Believers.' He is still with them. We stay away from them. I won't let Dianna and Troy go there after they went a few times."

"What happened to them," Dan asked?

"I don't want to say," Susan stated. "Just, it's not for us."

"Okay," Dan said. "I don't need to know. But Jay is still a Christian? Right?"

"He thinks he is the only Christian," Susan said with sadness.

"What?"

"They think they are the only true Christians and all others are false."

"Are you serious," Dan asked?

"Jay says we are heretics and luke-warm believers," Susan said. "He is convinced Jesus is going to spit us out of his mouth at the last judgment. He is completely immersed in the Lighthouse group. It has become his whole life. They have no fellowship with anyone who is not a member of their group. He even gives his paycheck to the church and they give him an allowance to live on. The strange thing is he is really happy, or he seems happy. He is always smiling. Ever other word out his mouth is 'the Lord.' It is not an environment I want Dianna to be exposed to. Things go on that aren't good. But I don't want to talk about it anymore. It's very disturbing to me."

"Okay," said Dan. "Let's give Jay a rest and talk about us." He hesitated for a few moments and said, "Susan I am falling in love with you. When my divorce is finalized I want you to think about you and me getting married. You don't have to answer me now because I want you to think about this. I know I am broken and still need lots of healing. You are the one I want to spend the rest of my life with."

Susan was not surprised by this declaration of intention to marry. She sensed it was coming for some time. She had tried to put the brakes on her feelings because she was afraid of being hurt if Dan stopped calling. She loved him. She said softly, "Yes I know." She hesitated, and then she pulled him to her and kissed him hard. Dan wasn't ready for this response, but he recovered quickly and kissed her back. They were kissing and caressing each other when they heard Dianna enter the front door. They jumped to opposite ends of the sofa.

They didn't fool Dianna for a second. "Alright, what's going on with you two?" she snapped.

"Nothing dear," Susan answered.

"Yuh, I believe that," Dianna said. "I can't leave you two alone for a minute. Do we have anything to eat?"

Dan and Susan started giggling. As Susan and Dianna went into the kitchen to make something for Dianna to eat Dan looked around at the photographs on the walls and on the mantle. There were many photos of Susan, Dianna, Susan's parents and siblings, nephews and nieces, and not one photo of Jay. Dan though this was normal for a divorced family but wondered if it was significant. He was curious about why Susan and Jay had separated but didn't want to probe too deeply. Susan never had said anything negative about Jay until today. So Jay was in some super Christian group and he had no use for Methodists. He decided to look up the Lighthouse Fellowship of Believers on the internet and find out what they were about.

Dan had more important things to think about than an ex-husband, however, was still trying to comprehend how Jesus was in the people at the soup kitchen. Why did he feel that presence so powerfully, he wondered? Then he remembered what Susan had told him, "Just as you do it to the least of these you do it to me." So serving the poor is serving Jesus? He asked Susan for a Bible and she told him to look at the Gospel of John chapter 13, and there he found the story of Jesus washing the feet of his disciples. It was clear in this text that the followers of Jesus are called to be servants. This was a new discovery to Dan because he was a product of the corporate world of business and the higher you climbed the more privileges you earned. In the business world you did not strive to become a servant. He was seeing Jesus as counter the values he had been taught all his life. This day, Dan's world turned upside down. He was forced to confront his preconceived attitudes about the poor. He was astonished to feel the presence of Christ in the menial task of serving soup. So Dan realized being a servant was the highest aspiration of a Christian. Susan had pointed out that Jesus had stated all these things clearly two thousand years before. Dan was convinced he needed to study the Bible more diligently in order to understand what it meant to be a follower of Jesus.

That week he called Reverend Bob and asked him what he could do to help prepare for next Saturday's soup kitchen. During the conversation Dan mentioned his concern about a lack of vegetables. Reverend Bob told him of a wholesale produce company that might donate some vegetables if he spoke to Tony and told him the produce was for Reverend Bob. So early Thursday morning Dan went to Caruso's Wholesale Produce and asked for Tony. Tony was in a small office in the refrigerated warehouse that contained crates of every kind of produce. Dan told him he was hoping for some vegetables for Reverend Bob's soup kitchen. Tony yelled for Mickey and ordered him to give Dan some donation for Reverend Bob. Mickey led Dan back into the warehouse past piles of cartons of fruits and vegetables. He tossed a fifty pound sack of carrots on a hand cart, and then he grabbed a box of lettuce and pitched that on top of the carrots. In a couple of minutes he had also piled potatoes, tomatoes, apples and leeks onto the cart. The loaded cart must have weighed over three hundred pounds, and Tony pushed it with ease to the loading dock. "Which is your truck," Mickey asked.

Dan said, "I'll pull it up to the dock."

Dan backed his Lexus up to the loading dock between the semi-trucks. The dock was almost five feet high so Mickey had to unload the cart and pile the cartons on the edge of the loading dock for Dan to lift them off the dock and load his car. The trunk was filled with three cartons and the rest went on his back seat. Dan realized several of the cartons were seeping fluids from the contents and this was not going to be good for his seat covers but he didn't have anything to protect his seat covers. He loaded his car and thanked Mickey. Mickey walked away laughing. He knew he was dealing with a novice. As he backed out he almost hit a van driven by a nun who was baking up to the loading dock.

When Dan took the food to Reverend Bob's church where they prepared the food it was about eight-thirty and the building was dark. As he was carrying the cartons of produce into the kitchen a man appeared from nowhere and stopped him. "What are you doing here?" he barked. Dan was not sure how to respond. This person had only a couple of teeth showing and had not shaved in a week. He was wearing pajama bottoms, untied gym shoes, and a winter coat. He looked like he had not slept in a long time.

After looking him over and wondering what gave this man the right to question him, Dan replied, "Vegetables for Reverend Bob."

"Let me help you," the man said. "Why aren't you using the hand truck? Those boxes are too heavy to be carrying in your arms. You gunna break your back."

"Thanks. I could use the help. I'm Dan."

"I'm Bill. I live here."

After they brought all the boxes into the kitchen, Bill invited Dan to have some coffee he had just brewed. Bill offered some pastries from a half crushed box of raspberry Danish. Dan asked where Reverend Bob was. Bill told him he would be coming soon. Bill asked Dan questions as if he was interviewing him for a position. Bill was evasive when Dan asked him questions about himself. The only information Dan got from Bill was he was from Kentucky and knew Reverend Bob a long time. Finally Reverend Bob arrived with his arms filled with bags of bread. He told Bill there was more in the van and if he was not too busy. Bill left to retrieve the bread. Reverend Bob was clearly surprised by the large amount of produce Dan had procured. Reverend Bob opened the cartons and inspected the contents. He was excited when he discovered the leeks. "These leeks will make the best dam onion soup you ever had!"

"How do you make onion soup out of leeks?" Dan asked him.

"We tell them it is onion soup," Reverend Bob, "because if we tell them it is leek soup they won't eat it."

"Why not?"

"Most of them have never had leeks," Reverend Bob said, "and they won't try something they don't know."

Dan told Reverend Bob he was bringing his girl friend and her daughter on Saturday. Reverend Bob smiled and mentioned they had a youth group from a church up North coming to help, and it was a good thing, because they would need all the help they could get preparing the meal. Dan asked what else they would be serving and Reverend Bob told him the group was bringing chicken. Dan commented he was going to try to find some donors to help support Reverend Bob's charity. That set Reverend Bob off.

"It's not charity," he said irritated. "Not in the way you mean it. If you were using the word in the original meaning of the word like its use in the King James Bible I wouldn't have a problem with it but I suspect you are saying charity as giving stuff away for the poor people who need our leftovers. That makes me sick. People getting rid of their old castoffs because they don't have room in their closets for more stuff, and they think they are so righteous! Real charity is an act of sacrificial love, and that is what it means in the King James Bible, like in 1 Corinthians 13 which is read at practically every wedding. It is not sentimental love it is the unconditional love of Jesus Christ which is very different than the needy self serving love of this world. The Agape love of Jesus is real "charitas" and that is costly. So I take the charity that I'm offered and we thank the people for it but I don't give that to the people I serve I try to give them something holy which is Christ's love. And that's not just about words. It's the deeds they need. Before you say you love them you better see if they are hungry first. You probably don't know what it is like to be on the streets with nothing; but before you feel sorry for these people you have to put something in their empty bellies, put a warm coat on them in the winter, find a place for them to sleep at night. That is my sermon! As Brother Saint Francis said, 'Preach always, and, if you must use words.' If you want to really follow Jesus you need to listen to people and stand with them and not over them. Don't think you know what they need until you learn to listen to them. Well that's what happens when you hang around an old preacher. How did you like the sermon?"

"That was powerful," Dan sheepishly replied. "I will be more careful using the word charity next time."

" Dan," Reverend Bob said, "you did a good job getting the produce."

When Dan left the church and opened his car door the smell of stale vegetable was overwhelming. He knew it was going to take him hours to clean his back seat and trunk to get the juice stains out.

Chapter 10 - Unlocked

Fordham Road is a dead end street on which Dan lives. There isn't much traffic, especially at the end where Dan's house is located. Mindy keeps an ear open for any cars or people that come down the street. She has a deep throaty bark, and Dan has learned her different emotions by the sounds she makes. He could be working in his office at the back of the house, and know by the warning wuff, concerned arf, or alarmed bark just what Mindy was feeling. Lately, he had tried to ignore her more frequent alarm barking because he was stressed out over his business problems. He dismissed it most of the time, but regrettably, had often found a delivery had been made to his door when she was giving the furious alarm. He occasionally noticed an older white sedan driving slowly by his house, turning around at the end of the street, and slowly driving back by. Dan didn't want to think he was paranoid, but someone was definitely checking him out. There were other troublesome signs that worried Dan. One time when he came home, Mindy was outside the house. He had left her in the house. He never left her outside, so how did she get out? When he checked the doors, everything was locked. Had he left a door unlocked? Dan decided to secure his home. He added deadbolts to the doors, changed the locks, and bought a close circuit camera system. Mark, from the group, came over and helped him install the system. Now he would have images recorded of anyone snooping around his yard. He wondered if this strange activity was related to the disappearance of his antique pistol collection.

Dan loved to cook and especially shined when Susan, Troy, and Dianna came. Dinner at Dan's had become a weekly affair he looked forward to. Tonight Dan was making stuffed chicken with penne, and a Greek salad. After dinner all four of them would watch a movie together on Dan's 52-inch flat screen TV. Dianna was such a responsible student that she would often bring her notebook computer and do her homework and while watching the movie.

When the doorbell rang and Dan opened the door, Troy rushed past him and to play with Mindy. They disappeared out the back door to romp. Dianna gave Dan a hug. This was the first hug she had ever offered him and he almost froze in her brief embrace. He was very fond of Dianna, but wondered if he- as the new boyfriend in her mother's life - was acceptable to her. This brief embrace told Dan she accepted him. He and Susan were careful to try not to show any physical signs of affection around Troy or Dianna. They knew Dianna did not approve of that stuff. Since Dianna quickly moved into the kitchen to inspect the dinner, Susan and Dan had a moment alone. Susan kissed Dan on the lips and he kissed her back. She had to push him away because he was not satisfied with just a couple of kisses.

"What did you make tonight," Susan asked?

"The menu is chicken, pasta, salad, and a surprise for dessert." Dan replied. "I hope you are hungry because I went a little overboard and there is enough for eight people. If you like it, you can take some home for your dinner tomorrow."

"I'm sure it will be delicious," Susan said as the two of them headed for the kitchen. "I know you don't like to eat left over's, but Dianna, Troy, and I love left over's. Anything you make, we will be happy to take with us. So what did you do today? Did you have the meeting with the lawyers?"

"Yes, which was not the highlight of my day," Dan answered. "It looks like we have everything worked out. They were talking about a court date in a couple of weeks, if we both sign the financial settlement."

Susan sensed some hurt in Dan and said, "Are you all right with the way things have turned out?"

"I can live with it. Whether my company will survive the hit is another question," Dan answered. This is about the worst experience of my life. I don't know how Donna can be so cold. Why has it taken me this long to finally get it? It is all about the money. She doesn't want anything to do with me. That's what really hurts more than the money. I will always care for her, but she has made it clear she wants nothing to do with me. All she wants is the money."

"Did you ask her about the pistols?" Susan inquired. "She never told you if she took them or not. She owes you an answer?"

"You should have been there," Dan said. "If looks could kill! I asked her in front of the suits, and she gave me this huge smile and said, 'If you have lost them, that's your problem.' I just can't figure out what happened to them," Dan said frustrated. "I know need to let it go, but I can't. I have contacted my insurance agent and he thinks I am covered for the loss on my home owner's policy. Those pistols are worth a lot of money. The insurance money on the loss of those pistols could save my business for awhile, anyway."

Troy came rushing into the room out of breath. He looked at his mother and wanted to say something but didn't speak. "What is it Troy?" she asked. "What happened?"

"Mom," he said, "I need to tell you something, but not here." He looked at Dan and turned away.

They went into the kitchen and Susan asked him again, "What's the matter?"

Troy looked her in the eye and exclaimed, "Dad!"

"What do you mean, 'Dad'?" She asked. "What about him?"

"He's parked down the street," he replied. "When he saw me looking at him he ducked down. Like, I don't know his car. Why is he here? Is he following us? Mom, what's going on?"

Susan searched for an answer and said, "Honestly, I don't know." They returned to Dan in the living room. Susan was trying to regain her composure and didn't want to alarm Dan. She decided it was better to not make an issue of this because she was uncertain what Dan might do. She would do anything to avoid a confrontation between Dan and Jay. She needed to protect her children and she needed to protect Dan from something that could turn quite ugly. She said, "Troy thought he saw something, and it scared him. He's okay now."

They went to the kitchen and everyone helped carry the food to the table. Susan hid her concern during dinner and pretended to be cheerful. Before the dinner was over she excused herself to use the bathroom and carefully looked out the front windows down the street. There was no old white Honda anywhere. It was gone. She knew Troy was not mistaken.

After dinner they all were treated to homemade cookies and cream ice cream. It was the kids favorite. Dan and Susan selected a movie for the kids to watch, and Dan and Susan sat in the dining room and talked over coffee. Susan told Dan how some women from the church had come to her when she and Jay were separated. They had given her unconditional love and support, and one saint even offered her financial assistance. She told Dan she never could have gone through the divorce without her friends. It was hell, but her sisters in Christ got her through it. She thanked God for their prayers. The guilt of failing in marriage and breaking up their family was more than she could bear alone. She believed God was against divorce, but she felt they were in real danger because Jay was not a well person. She knew Jesus forgave her. Pastor Andy initially talked her into going to marriage counseling with Jay. That was a disaster. Jay exploded at the second counseling session and threatened the life of the psychologist. Later in a private conversation with the psychologist even suggested moving the family to a safe house. After that, Pastor Andy became a strong ally in her decision to end the marriage. They didn't move away. She just wanted Jay to leave them alone. The court had granted her custody of the children and he had very limited visitation. There were problems every time he took the children and she worried he might take off someday with the kids. She had given up on child support because he'd rather serve jail time than pay. He didn't have any money anyways because he gave everything to his church. Susan stated that she didn't hate Jay, she truly cared about him, but she knew she couldn't have anything to do with him. She hoped the kids would never allow him to abduct them.

Dan was listening intently as Susan described the break-up of her marriage to him. He was deeply sympathetic and appreciated the fact that Susan had confided in him. He knew she was sparing him the sordid details of the relationship. But he didn't really want to know much more. He was feeling very protective of Susan and her children and was curious about what was going on in Jay's head. Dan knew Susan was a very desirable, compassionate, intelligent, and capable woman ,and he couldn't imagine what was Jay thinking driving her away? He wondered how dangerous was Jay? Dan was not a violent man, but he would do what was necessary to protect Susan and her children if it ever came to that.

After the movie was over, Susan took Troy and Dianna home. Dan thought about the things he had learned about Jay. He went around the house and checked his locks and then he watched replays of his security cameras. Other than a few brief glimpses of a deer in the backyard, there was nothing unusual to see. He had trouble going to sleep that night. Dan usually prayed before he went to sleep, but this night he was so troubled, he neglected to pray. He had a vivid dream of being stalked in his own house. Mindy had her throat slit open, and he was carrying her lifeless corpse down the stairs to the basement to take her into the backyard to bury her. In the basement he saw a dark figure breaking into his gun cabinet. He dropped Mindy and grabbed the arm of the man loading his rifle. He was trying to wrestle the rifle away from the man and it went off. That is when he suddenly awoke. He was sweating. For a moment he wondered if he was still locked in mortal combat or if this was it just a dream. He had trouble going back to sleep because every time he began to drift into sleep the dream battle started where it left off. It was a bad night.

That morning Dan prayed hard. He asked Jesus to take the violent thoughts from his mind. He asked Jesus to show him what to do. He read his Bible and pondered over passages about "turning the other cheek." He read how Jesus told Pilate "he could summon an army of ten thousand angels" and didn't. On the contrary, Dan knew he was capable of anything to defend the people he loved. Would Jesus condemn him for protecting Susan? He called Peter and told him he wanted to meet him for lunch because he had something he urgently needed to talk about. Dan was worried if he was capable of committing an unforgivable sin and losing his salvation.

Peter met him at their favorite hamburger place, which happened to be a bar in an obscure part of town. The menu was severely limited, but that didn't matter because people came here for the burgers, which were superb. Dan told Peter he was struggling with feeling of anger toward his girlfriend's ex-husband and he was afraid he could lose his salvation if he did something violent; even though it would be to protect Susan. Dan had searched the New Testament and found nothing to excuse violence. Quite the opposite he found plenty of teachings by Jesus advocating pacifism. He asked Peter what Peter would do?

Peter told him this was a question that has been debated in Christianity for two thousand years. He explained to him Saint Augustine's theory of a "just war" and how that was applicable to his dilemma. In fairness, Peter also told Dan about several of the Christian groups that were strict pacifists like the Quakers and Mennonites. According to Peter, Dan was going to have to pray about it and be open to the guidance of the Holy Spirit to determine what he was called by God to do. Without much hesitation Dan answered he knew in his heart what he would do. He told Peter he would never let anyone harm Susan or her children. He would do what had to be done to stop an attack. He would not initiate that action.

Peter asked, "Are you sure?"

"There is no doubt in my mind God would want me to protect my loved ones," Dan snapped back. "If I didn't do everything I could humanly do to keep someone from harming then, I couldn't live with myself. I guess I am just going to have to believe that God would understand why I did it. Is this something God could never forgive?"

"Is there anything God cannot forgive?" Peter responded. "How big is God's mercy? Really think about it. When Jesus hung on the cross, looking down on the people who he had come to save, what did he do? He said, "Father forgive them for they know not what they do." These people where the very ones mocking him and killing him. He forgave them and he forgave you from that cross. What kind of a sinner do you think you are? Do you think your sin is too big for Jesus to forgive? Dan, you know you belong to the Good Shepherd and he will never let you go. Do the very best you can to avoid sin, and put your trust in our most capable Savior."

Dan heard what Peter was saying about Jesus and his salvation. He decided he was not going to worry about his salvation. He tried to remember the cross whenever he had doubts about his eternal fate. The one absolute truth in his life was his heart's desire to belong to Jesus. There is nothing in the world that was going to change that. Every time the evil one came at him with anxieties about his faith, Dan looked to the cross and remembered he belonged to Lord Jesus. He could never betray what God had done for him to win his salvation. Dan had no idea what scheme was being devised to annihilate his faith.

Chapter 11 - Down, but not Out

The routine divorce proceeding was surreal from Dan's perspective. The courtroom held a Judge, court recorder, two attorneys, Dan, Donna, and more than four dozen empty chairs. The entire proceeding lasted a few minutes and the Judge announced the divorce decree would be issued in an hour. The financial settlement had taken weeks to mediate, was now signed by both parties, and the rest was just a formality. A marriage that had lasted years was wiped away in minutes. Dan walked down the courthouse steps in a daze. He thought about the day they had walked up these same steps to get the marriage license, and how happy and excited they were. The wedding was beautiful, and Donna was radiant in her wedding dress. He told everyone he was the luckiest man alive to marry Donna. When they exchanged marriage vows they both became teary eyed. He kept wondering how love slips away? Donna had made it explicitly clear she did not love him and wanted a divorce. He knew he would always love her; but, now, he had to let her go. He could not force her to love him. He couldn't force her to stay married to him. He had prayed and prayed that God would change her mind, but nothing changed. *Why would God not change her mind?* Dan wondered. *Was his prayer not what God wanted? Why didn't God answer his prayer?* He walked past his car lost in a whirlwind of thought.

The best thing that had come from all of this pain was this relationship with Jesus. He had called out to Jesus, and had been given a whole new heart and understanding about his life. It was a heavy price to pay, but he now believed any pain was worth enduring for the sake of knowing Jesus. He knew that it was his brokenness from being rejected by Donna that drove him to seek Jesus. He had been knocked down, and Jesus had lifted him up. In a weird way that catastrophe was a gift. *Did God plan it that way?* Dan wondered to himself. *Do all things work for God's good purpose for those who love God?*

That afternoon he called Susan and told her about the divorce being final. She said she would pray for him. Susan had been through the same experience and could relate to what he must be going through. She had experienced the guilt and self recriminations, and knew their power to drive a person crazy. She had also experienced the shame of a failed marriage, and how the breaking the marriage vows was sinful. Fortunately for Dan there were no children to complicate the divorce. The welfare of children makes divorce much more difficult. Dan prayed to God to forgive him for all that he had done to contribute to the divorce and he prayed for Donna. He had tried to speak to her about his new found faith in Jesus. She was not dismissive, but she was clearly hostile to his attempt to witness to her. He realized it was not because Donna was a bad person; rather she was not receptive to him. He prayed someone else would tell her about Jesus, and she would listen to them.

Dan threw himself into his work. The furniture import busness was in jeopardy because of the financial settlement with Donna. He was scrambling to increase his cash flow to meet his bills.

When his insurance agent called him and told him the good news about the claim for the antique pistols being settled, he couldn't believe it. Over a period of thirty years he had searched for civil war era pistols and acquired twenty -six fine pieces. There are many counterfeit reproductions available, and he was meticulous in authenticating each gun before he bought it. The difference between an authentic piece and a reproduction could be miniscule, so he became expert in spotting the difference. He always assumed they would appreciate in value over time, but he did not realize how much they had increased in worth. The agent told him his collection was worth one hundred and thirty-two thousand, four hundred dollars. The check had been authorized. He was asked if he wanted it mailed, or did he want to pick it up? He told the agent he would be by tomorrow to get the check. The pistols had tripled in value from what he had spent on them. Now he could stop juggling his bills and invest in his business. That week he took Susan to the best restaurant in the city for a celebration. He told Susan he regretted the theft of his pistols, but this money was going to save his business. "God works in mysterious ways," Susan said.

Things were beginingg to get better for Dan. He was entertaining fantasies of marrying Susan. He even started looking on the internet about honeymoon vacations in exotic parts of the world. He couldn't help himself thinking about considering a honeymoon which would put him in a location to find a new source of exotic furnishings. What would Susan think about a honeymoon in Sri Lanka, Indonesia or Vietnam? Europe was too expensive for new furniture because of the low value of the dollar, and he wasn't interested in dealing in antique reproductions. He had the money to invest in a business trip and that would be a business tax deduction if he combined it with a honeymoon. He decided to just explain it to Susan that way and she would understand the reasoning.

Everything was going good when he got the phone call from Jay. Jay called him to ask for a meeting to discuss a matter of great importance. Dan asked if they could talk about it over the phone. Jay was insistent they had to meet, and it was not something he would talk about on the phone. So they arranged a meeting at a fast food restaurant for that afternoon. Dan recognized the white sedan in the parking lot when he drove in to meet Jay. As he entered the restaurant, Jay stood up and waved Dan to him. Dan didn't know what Jay looked like but Jay obviously recognized Dan immediately. Jay was strikingly handsome, in spite of his shabby clothes. He had an intense stare and never took his eyes off Dan. Dan introduced himself and Jay responded, "I know you."

"So what's up?" Dan asked. "I was wondering if we would meet. You know about my dating Susan?"

Jay wore a blank expression and stated, "It's not Susan I want to talk about. You are here because of what you are doing to my children, Troy and Dianna. I am their father, and it is my duty to raise them according to the law of man and of God. You may be naïve enough to think you can ingratiate yourself into their lives because of your having relations with my wife, but you are sadly mistaken." Jay's lips belied a slight smile as he continued, "There is nothing on this sick little planet that will come between me and my children. Susan has taken it upon herself to keep those children from me as much as possible, but the Lord will prevail. It is best for you and all parties concerned that you leave them alone."

"I'm not sure what you are talking about," Dan said before he was interrupted.

"Let's not play games," Jay said, "you know exactly what I am talking about. You might think you can fool people by taking them to the soup kitchen. That is not going to work on me. I know the whole deal."

Now Dan interrupted Jay, "And what's wrong with the soup kitchen?"

"You make this big show of feeding some lost souls some leftovers," Jay sneered, "and you call yourselves Christians. That con doesn't fool us for a second. When Jesus comes he knows who you are! He is not conned like you think. We have seen this show of the hypocrites before, and Jesus told them, "woe to you hypocrites! You white washed tombs." The Lord knows his own. You and your, so called, church, and it's works righteousness, is but a filthy rag before the Lord. These works will not save you from the wrath to come!"

Dan was not expecting this attack. He looked at his coffee and then back at Jay. He paused for a moment and then said, "So you object to feeding the poor? Didn't Jesus feed the hungry?"

"Jesus fed with the word of life. You know he declared the poor will always be with us," Jay retorted. "The people you enable in their depravity need a Savior, not soup. You use them to deceive yourself into thinking you can buy your way into heaven. Do you think you can play the Lord for a fool? We know your kind. My church has been battling for the true salvation of souls for centuries and your kind follows Lucifer. He is the ruler of this world. You follow the heretics that lead the sheep astray. Keep

Troy and Dianna away from the soup kitchen and that hypocrite, Pastor Bob. He's an angel from hell. We know him."

Dan had the thought that he was in another universe talking with Jay. Was Jay a mad man or could he be a prophet? What did Jay know that he didn't know? He clearly was a person of strong religious convictions. Is this all delusional or is there any truth to his rant? He was repulsed and intrigued at the same time. Dan wanted to run away from this zealot, but he also wanted to hear more. Dan asked, "Where is this church of yours?"

Jay looked intensely into Dan's eyes, and said, "When you seek his face he will come to you. We are worldwide. If you come to know the truth we are on Liberty Street where it crosses Oak Street. The Saturday service is for visitors and you would be blessed to come to the true worship of the Lord."

Dan belatedly realized some of the counter help were staring at them. They had not ordered anything. The conversation between the two men was not pleasant to watch. Dan said he would consider visiting the church and made an excuse to leave.

"You still have time to be saved," Jay said. "There is not much time left for this world. He is coming soon. He will judge the hypocrites and his wrath will consume them. May God have mercy on your soul."

As Dan pulled out of the parking lot he was startled to see Jay smiling and waving goodbye to him. Somewhere in the conversation he must have changed Jay's mind and turned from being an enemy to a friend, he thought. He was completely wrong. Jay had his own ideas, and Dan was not a friend in any way, shape, or form. Dan was a new Christian and was insecure in what doctrine he believed. He had a firm belief in Jesus Christ as his Savior. He believed because of his personal experience. His personal experience was supported by the testimony of the Holy Scripture. All of this was backed up by the community of believers at Hartwell Church. The numerous doctrines that various denominations taught were confusing to him. He was determined to find the right doctrine because he didn't want to believe in anything false. How was he to know what was was true and who was right? That question kept playing with his mind. Dan wanted a perfect faith with no room for doubts.

His gut told him that Reverend Bob was the real deal. He felt the ministry to the poor was authentic Christ-like behavior. He felt confident in Reverend Andy's teaching and preaching. The men in his support group were doing the best they could do to consciously follow the teachings of Jesus as they understood them. But was that enough? They were all flawed human beings. Is there a perfect faith? That is what Dan asked himself after meeting Jay. From what Susan had told him about Jay's faith and after his encounter with Jay in person, he wondered if there something he was missing in his faith. Jay had no doubts. His faith seemed so absolutely certain. He even knew things that were never discussed at Hartwell Church, like the coming of Christ. Was this the mark of a genuine believer? Jay would never tell an off color joke. He would never touch alcohol. Jay had no ambiguity in his faith. Dan wondered if that was the test of a real disciple of Jesus Christ.

He called Mark the science teacher because he respected his intellect and his faith. He asked Mark if he would go with him to the Saturday evening service at the church Jay attended. Mark said he could go with him. Mark didn't know anything about the Lighthouse Fellowship of Believers and was curious why Dan wanted to go to this church. Dan evaded the question and said he was just curious. So they agreed to go that next Saturday. Dan had thought about asking Peter, but didn't want to hurt Peter's feelings by looking at another church. Peter had led him to Hartwell Church and was very invested there. Mark could be more objective.

Dan had never heard of spiritual discernment, but the Holy Spirit was watching over him. The Spirit had put the idea of asking Mark to accompany him. The Holy Spirit never forces anyone to do anything, but the Holy Spirit was alive in Dan's life suggesting the course of his journey of faith. Dan had good instincts much of the time; but he was also human. There were base urges to keep struggling with his new, Christ-like self. Dan was aware of this conflict in some areas. In some parts of his life he was completely clueless what was conflicting. Dan wanted his faith to be perfect, complete, and without flaw like a beautifully crafted piece of furniture. Dan was anxious to find doctrinal perfection. Dan was sufficiently immature as a Christian to not appreciate the mysteries of the faith. Dan did not appreciate the value of doubts. What was more dangerous was Dan was compelled by his pride to think he could know everything. He secretly hoped he would be favored by God for his intellectual acuity. This was leading him to a crash course in humility. That was a lesson Dan was going to have to learn experientially.

Chapter 12 - What is Truth?

Mark picked Dan up on Saturday afternoon so they could attend Jay's church. When they arrived at the address, it was not readily apparent amongst the old storefronts which building housed the church. Dan spotted the hand painted sign on the window of one of the storefront which read Lighthouse Fellowship of Believers. The windows were all covered, and it wasn't clear whether the building was even open. Mark and Dan tentatively opened the door and went inside, hoping that they were going to meet up with Jay. A slightly built attractive young woman came towards them and gave them a very extravagant greeting. They asked about Jay. She informed them she had not seen him. The room was set up with folding chairs facing a stage where a band was busy setting up their instruments. There were two small groups of people sitting and standing around engaged in conversation. In the back of the room there was a large projection screen that had seen better days. The young woman introduced herself as Lacey. She ushered them forward to the front of the room near the band and asked them to make themselves at home. Mark and Dan sat down and looked around the room, watching as new people arrived, and wondering what they were doing there. After a long time the musicians stopped fiddling around with all the wires and knobs and they started warming up on their instruments. The mess of wires on the platform looked like long skinny black snakes. The huge speakers were piled atop one another.

The musicians looked more like heavy metal devotees than traditional Christian musicians. When they began playing it was evident they were heavy metal musicians, but the words they sang were Christian. Dan was almost knocked out of his chair by the volume of the music. The bass notes vibrated through the floor, chairs, and the whole building. Mark and Dan repositioned themselves further back from the speakers. More people were entering the room and sitting down. Dan had been to rock concerts before, but never one that was billed as church. The songs were trashing the devil and praising God. Some people got up and swayed and danced to the music. More and more people were coming into the building and people began shouting praises. This was a side of Christianity Dan never knew existed. After about twenty minutes the music stopped while the lead singer gave a long prayer. Dan was fascinated by the way he prayed. It was raw and deeply emotional. Dan was impressed with his sincerity. The music resumed and the seventy or more people gathered started to really get into it. People were jumping, shouting, and falling to the floor. Dan felt conspicuous as he and Mark sat motionless in the frenzy of this highly charged atmosphere. Finally, the music stopped and a young man in jeans and faded flannel shirt took a microphone and started preaching. The message was very complicated and convoluted so it was difficult for Dan to follow. The preacher knew his Bible very well and often cited chapter and verse in his sermon. As best as Dan could follow the preacher, he was warning them the rapture was coming soon and they must be ready. Those left behind would suffer a time of horrible torment led by a world-wide government presided over by the anti-Christ. He frequently mentioned signs in the book of Daniel and the book of Revelation. Many of the audience members agreed with the preacher and yelled their approval and encouragement. As the preacher reached the conclusion of his sermon; he made a passionate appeal for those who wanted to be saved from the hell to come. He insisted they must come forward and prostrate themselves before the Lord and beg God for mercy to spare them from the wrath that was coming.

At first only a few people came to the front and lay on the floor crying out for God to save them. The preacher shouted his previous warning. Immediately others followed and soon everyone except Dan and Mark was lying on the floor begging God to save them. Dan couldn't stand sitting there any longer and he went forward and prostrated himself in the mass of people. Dan shouted for God to save him. He was caught up in the hysteria of the cacophonous prayers around him. The preacher was exhorting them to beg God with all their hearts. He told them God demanded they cry out with all their might. The noise of the people screaming was deafening. Eventually the preacher became quiet, and the people who were exhausted from their exertions of prayer calmed down. As the room became still the band began to play softly. The preacher invited people to raise their hands for prayers of healing. When a hand was raised several persons would go to that individual and lay hands upon them and pray for them. They were mostly praying in tongues and shouting praises. Dan decided to return to his seat and watch what was unfolding.

Mark was still sitting were Dan had left him. They watched as people who had raised their hands were prayed over, and then they would leap up and announced their healing. This was intensely emotional, and accompanied with tears and wailing. By the intensity of their feeling, it was evident they were completely sincere. Dan was amazed by what was happening right in front of him. He felt captivated by these signs of incredible faith and presence of the Holy Spirit. As he experienced this more intense expression of faith, Dan wondered if this was more authentic than what he was experiencing at Hartwell Church? These were the kind of thoughts Dan was having when Jay showed up. Mark and Dan had not seen Jay all evening, but when the service was about over he came and sat behind them. Jay began studying Mark. Jay was eager to engage Dan in conversation, but was apparently reluctant to do so in the company of Mark. Mark had not gone forward and prostrated himself and had not responded to the call for individual prayer. Secretly Jay had been observing them from a distance for some time. Finally, Jay asked Dan if he had felt the Holy Spirit?

"This was new to me," Dan answered. "Is this service like this every week? It was powerful! The band kind of put me off at first, but I could see how people really got into it. The healings were awesome."

"You have no idea of the power of the Spirit," Jay replied, "when you know the Lord."

"I appreciate your inviting me here," Dan said, "because I just had no idea it could be like this."

"That's what I wanted you to see for yourself," Jay responded. "Those lukewarm fools at Hartwell would keep this from you. You have been lost in their lies." Jay looked at Mark with a penetrating glare.

Mark stood up. He looked at Jay and interrupted him, "Dan and I were just about to go. Thanks for the opportunity to worship with your church. It has been interesting, but we better be going now." Mark headed for the door. Dan followed.

Jay held them with his eyes as they walked out the door. Dan turned to Mark and asked him why he was in such a hurry to leave. Mark said he wanted to talk about the service, but maybe they should stop somewhere and have coffee to discuss it. They agreed to stop at a Aunt Maudie's coffee shop on the way home. There was an awkward silence in the car between Dan and Mark. Dan's mind was racing with questions for Mark. Dan could sense Mark was deeply troubled, but had no idea what was bothering him.

When they had settled into the booth at the coffee shop, Dan asked, "So, Mark, what's up? You seem to be holding something back. Why don't you say what you've got to say?"

That was all the invitation Mark needed. "Dan," he began, "tonight was possibly something new for you. It is not new for me. I was raised in a church with similar practices to the one we just attended. There is nothing wrong with the way they demonstrate their faith so fervently. In many ways I admire them and how uninhibited they do their thing. Because I was raised in that kind of church, I am also aware of many things that make me uncomfortable which you may not be aware of. There were just too many red flags for me. I can appreciate their enthusiasm but it is not for me anymore. The more I studied science the more questions I had about their literal interpretation of the Bible. It got to the point where I was no longer welcome with a less literal understanding based in science."

None of Mark's explanation was very satisfactory to Dan. He seemed to be alluding to things that made him uncomfortable.

What does that have to do with me? Dan wondered. If something unpleasant happen to Mark when he was younger at his church, why judge Jay's church based by what had happened elsewhere?

Later, at home, Dan thought about Mark. He knew Mark had a powerful intellect and a strong faith as well. He had seen several examples of it in action. He wondered how could a man of his faith and intelligence be so narrow-minded and fail to see the virtue of the worship they had just witnessed! Dan, himself, was still enthralled by his experience of the Spirit.

He let Mindy out the back door and was about to accompany her for a walk in the back yard for some fresh night air when the phone rang. It was Susan and she asked if she could come over. This was uncharacteristic of Susan, so Dan asked her if everything was okay. She assured him she just wanted to see him and everything was fine.

Dan made some hot tea for Susan and prepared it on a large, hand-painted lacquered tray he had brought back from China. They kissed when Susan entered the house. Dan served her tea and cookies as they sat on the sofa in the living room. Susan didn't hesitate to initiate the conversation. This was surprising to Dan because she was usually reserved. She told Dan she had been worried about him going to church with Jay. She had been praying for him the whole time, and she was thankful to God he was home safe. Dan told her it was a great worship service and he had been deeply moved by the power of the Holy Spirit. He told her Mark had gone with him, and he was disappointed that Mark had some baggage which kept him from getting into the spirit of the worship.

"Dan," Susan said cautiously, "I think you're missing something here. There's more going on than you know." Dan, however, was still thinking about the healings and the praise. He completely missed what Susan was trying to say to him. Susan did not want to tell Dan some very ugly things about the past, but she realized it was the only way to get through to him. Susan reluctantly was determined to tell Dan some secrets that she has kept to herself for years.

"Dan, this is very hard for me," Susan began, "so just let me speak. It would be better if you don't ask questions. You are going to hear things I was never going to talk about with anyone. When Jay and I married, I thought we were going to live happily ever after. We were both Christians and we were very involved at Hartwell church. People must have seen us as the perfectly happy Christian couple. That was what I wanted. It was important to us that we put up that appearance. Jay is a perfectionist, and he wanted us to be perfect in everything. He is also very controlling. We became active in everything that happened at the church. Practically every time the doors were opened we were there. Our life revolved around our jobs and church. That was it. But it was never enough for Jay. He avoids direct confrontation but he was very critical of the church and the way things were run. He would never speak directly to the people at the church with whom he disagreed, but he would often unload on me. I was always in the position of defending people and decisions with which he disagreed. Finally he got so agitated over a discussion about homosexuality that he pulled us out of the church. Meanwhile, he was becoming obsessed with some teachings about the end times he learned on the internet. Based on these teachings, he decided Hartwell was teaching complete heresy."

"We started going to conservative churches but there was always something or someone who would set him off, and we would move onto another church. By this time the kids were old enough for Sunday school, they wanted some stability. They would start making friends at a church and then have the rug pulled out from under them."

"Jay was laid off from his job. He had a lot of trouble finding another job. We had financial problems. We weren't meeting our obligations. There was tension at home. He was always a good father, but the kids were being affected by the constant tension over money. Jay became more and more convinced the world was against him. I begged him to see a counselor but he didn't believe in that stuff. When I stopped going along with his church shopping and his other obsessions, he accused me of infidelity.

That was more than I could bear. I asked him to leave if he really believed I was a whore. He packed up and left. Even after he left I still was hoping he was just going through a bad time and we would work it out. He moved back home a few times, then there would be an explosion, and he would move out." Dan discreetly poured more hot tea in their cups. "Jay was not helping with the expenses. I was having trouble paying the bills. It began to be clear to me that I needed him to contribute to the household expenses, but he wasn't going to do that unless I submitted to him totally. That was not about to happen. Some friends of mine at school advised me to consult an attorney and I did. When I told Jay I was talking to an attorney about him helping with the support of the children-that apparently was the turning point for him. He began threatening me. I even was told by the attorney to get a restraining order against him. I didn't do it, but maybe I should have."

"There were some horrible scenes. It was so bad the police were called by our neighbors twice. Can you imagine how humiliating that was for me and the kids? The kids and I had returned to Hartwell Church. I was talking with Pastor Andy. He suggested a marriage counselor. That was a disaster. Jay threatened the counselor. That's when I began talking to the attorney about divorce. What was wrong with Jay was not something I could deal with anymore. I loved him but he was becoming dangerous to me. He took the kids every week for overnight stays. After a while the kids were behaving strangely and I was concerned about them. They finally told me about things with Jay and his new church that were very upsetting. I don't want to go into detail, but let me tell you a little bit. Some of the elders at his church determined that my children were under the influence of Satan, and Satan needed to be exorcised. They were laying hands on them with teams of the older men, and yelling at the demons to leave them. Troy and Dianna were coming home to me very upset. My children-my children!-were told I was a whore and in league with the devil. They were not supposed to talk with me. They had been told to demand to live with their father."

"That's when I put restrictions on visitation. That, however, only made things worse. Finally the divorce was completed and Jay was given very limited visitation. Since then, he barely speaks to me. I know he stalks me and the kids. He has contacted you now. What he is planning is what worries me. He doesn't want you to be a part of Troy or Dianna's lives. He is going to pull something. That is why he got you to his church. He is trying to draw you in, and then what?"

Dan was confused. He knew deep down in his soul that Susan had told him the truth. Knowing Susan as he did, he knew she had understated things. Susan never wanted to say anything derogatory about anyone. But the church's worship service he'd just attended, that wasn't a threat, was it? He thought it was a step toward reconciliation with Jay. Was the invitation to church part of a plot in Jay's mind? Dan remembered the thinly veiled threats at the restaurant that Jay had made. Dan realized he might be playing with a man who was not to be taken lightly. Is it possible that Jay was using his church as a cover for something sinister? Susan certainly knew what Jay was capable of.

Chapter 13 - The True Church

When the phone rang, Dan didn't recognize the phone number on his cell phone. He answered the call and was surprised it was Jay. Jay didn't waste any time getting to the point. He said, "Are you ready to come to our church Wednesday night? You only saw our worship for seekers. Wednesday night is for the committed believers. You need to decide if you are giving yourself to a dead church or are you ready to be a disciple of the Lord? Are you coming or not?"

Dan was conflicted, but remembered he had been warned by Susan that there was a hidden agenda with Jay. He was reluctant to be lured into Jay's unknown plot. "I can't go this time," He answered, " I need more time to think about things. So thanks for the invitation, but not now." The call went silent and the screen on his cell phone told him the connection was broken. Dan stared at the phone for a minute. He knew in his heart he probably would not be invited again. The tone in Jay's voice made it clear it was all or nothing.

There was something far more pressing in Dan's mind at the moment than Jay's invitation. He was thinking about formally asking Susan to marry him, and hopefully setting a date for the wedding. He had told Susan of his intentions. She was responsive to the proposition, but he had not formally proposed. They were not engaged. He had not even bought an engagement ring. They had not dared to go further at that time because his divorce had not been finalized. Now that he had been divorced for a couple of months, it was time to move forward. There was also the passion he had for Susan, and he wanted to consummate their love. Susan had made it clear this would only happen when they were married. Dan was ready to love Susan with all his being. He could protect her from harm, and they would make a new home for the children.

Sunday after church, Dan invited Susan for lunch at a Chinese restaurant that served dim sum on the weekends. Dan had developed a great liking for dim sum when he was in Hong Kong, and he had searched for a Chinese restaurant that served it where they lived. Dan told Susan he needed to speak to her about something personal and he thought it would be better if the children didn't come. He felt guilty about excluding Troy and Dianna, but it was appropriate for what he was planning. After they sat down at the restaurant, Dan and Susan filled out the paper menu checking off the eight different exotic dim sum dishes they would eat. The owner of the restaurant, Mrs. Wong, came by the table and chatted with Dan. Mrs. Wong knew Dan and appreciated his enjoyment of dim sum and his willingness to try new dishes. What Susan didn't know was that Dan and Mrs. Wong had been in contact the day before, and planned a surprise for Susan. After the steamed shrimp dumplings arrived and several other dishes Mrs. Wong presented Susan with a special plate of food shaped like flowers. In the center of the flowers was a small white silk box. "What's this?" Susan said.

Dan looked into her eyes and said, "Why don't you open it?" Susan opened the little silk-covered box and tears came to her eyes. It was an extravagantly beautiful diamond ring. "Susan will you be my wife," Dan asked?

"Yes, Dan," Susan said. "You know I will." Dan tried not to cry, but couldn't help himself. Mrs. Wong was watching from a distance and became teary eyed. She brought them her wonderful coconut buns. This was the first time Mrs. Wong had served a diamond ring. Dan began asking Susan what she wanted for a wedding and when they could be married. They talked about how they would tell the children. They had no trouble deciding about asking Pastor Andy to perform the service at Hartwell Church. After some discussion, they concluded there was no necessity in having a long engagement so they determined to be married in three months if the pastor and church were available. Susan wondered if it was appropriate to ask Dianna to be a bride's maid.

They started talking about the honeymoon. Dan was thinking about something exotic like Thailand or Sri Lanka. Susan told him he was being too extravagant and impractical. They needed to plan the honeymoon around her spring break from teaching because she couldn't get more than that one week off from her job. Traveling half way round the world was not going to work with the eight or nine days she would have off. She suggested they go somewhere in the Caribbean because it was much closer and they could save money on airfare by not going so far. Dan hadn't considered this. When he had thought about their honeymoon before talking it over with Susan, he had thought he might combine the honeymoon with a bit of business so he could write off some of the expenses. They agreed to look into possible locations for a honeymoon in the Caribbean. If they could time the wedding for a Saturday at the beginning of Susan's Spring break they might get a flight out for that Saturday or Sunday. Susan had a sister who could stay with the kids and Mindy could stay at Susan's house. They stayed and talked at the Chinese restaurant for three hours. They drank so much jasmine tea they were floating in. Even the fortune cookies were auspicious. Dan's fortune read, "You will find your heart's desire soon." Susan's cookie read, "Take advantage of opportunity for future success."

That afternoon, after Dan dropped Susan home, Dan went into his office and thought about the honeymoon. Dan had been to Mexico but not to the Caribbean islands. He was interested in something unusual and exotic, but not too challenging. That was when he thought about Mark. He recalled Mark had done many mission trips with youth groups in Central America. Perhaps Mark could give him some recommendations based on his experiences. When he called Mark he found Mark eager to share his knowledge about the places he had visited. Mark also wanted to talk to Dan about the worship experience they had shared together at Jay's church. Mark invited Dan to meet at his house. He had only one reservation, and that was the chaos of his home because he had four teenage sons.

Two days later Dan was at Mark's house hoping for some direction about what would be a unique honeymoon destination in the Caribbean. Fortunately Mark's boys were engaged in activities away from home. Mark had given this considerable thought and was prepared to advise Dan. The meeting began with Dan giving a rambling summary of all the places he had looked at on the internet. He had checked out sites from Aruba to Costa Rica and most places in between. Dan said every website had beautiful pictures and every amenity. It was almost impossible to choose. Mark said he had asked himself if he was taking his wife on a honeymoon, where would he want to spend that time with her? Mark also asked if they had the perfect honeymoon, what would that look like? Dan thought about it and said, "A beautiful wooden house right on the beach with just a few neighbors. No pressure to dress up or do anything. Maybe we would have some access to snorkeling or sailing. Great fresh seafood cooked by a local person is a must. Palm trees, white sand, and clear blue Caribbean water is all we want. Is that asking too much?"

"I know just the place," Mark replied. "We have taken a couple trips to a village that is off the beaten path in Belize called Hopkins. It is a small village right on the ocean, and there is a resort owned by this wonderful Dutch couple who rent a few cabanas on stilts built on the beach. They have a local woman who cooks whatever is the fresh catch that day from the ocean. The prices are really reasonable. They will arrange scuba diving, sailing, snorkeling, or whatever you want. The boat will come right to the beach in front of your house. If you scuba, this is a great location because Belize has the second biggest reef system in the world. The best part is Belize is an English-speaking country so you can interact with the local people without any problems. If this interests you, the name of the place is "Coconuts Cabanas." You can look them up on the internet. That is the name of their website, and if you want to make reservations, you can do it on their website. They are pretty booked up, so you need to get on it if you are interested. Do you want some other recommendations?"

"That sounds perfect!" Dan answered. "This is just what we had in mind. We just want to hang out in marital bliss on the beach. I'm going to tell Susan about it and we'll look at the website together. It's amazing that you knew about this place. The choices are overwhelming. Having someone who has been there makes all the difference. I'm so glad I asked you."

"Dan, it is my pleasure to help you and Susan any way I can," Mark responded. "You know many of us hold you in high regard. We all love Susan. Seeing you and Susan happy together and now getting married is a great joy for the whole church. Susan has been through enough. We have been through some hard times with Jay. Susan deserves some happiness. You are good for each other. Dianna and Troy need a stable father. God has blessed all of you by finding each other."

Mark asked Dan if he wanted some coffee. Mark got the coffee and sat down again with Dan. "Dan, there is something I want to tell you if you don't mind changing the subject for a little while."

"No problem," said Dan. "What is it?"

"I need to explain to you why I was so sullen the night we went to Jay's church," Mark answered. "This is what I have wanted to tell you. The worship we visited was much like the church I grew up in. It has some bad associations for me. I do not disapprove or judge the way they worshipped. It has nothing to do with that kind of worship. In many ways it is admirable. I do miss some of that enthusiastic demonstration of the gifts of the Holy Spirit." Mark hesitated for a moment and then continued. " The church I attended growing up had very rigid doctrine and views of the Bible. There was no room for different views or even questioning the things they taught. When I began studying science in high school I started asking questions which eventually led to me being thrown out of the church. I was told I was going to hell and was ostracized by members of the church including several relatives. It was very painful for a young person but it was not possible for me to submit to their 'our way or the highway' attitudes."

"It is not just them that I have a problem with. It is the people who have to be right all the time. I was equally at odds with some professors I had at the university who were just as self righteous, but from the opposite position. Science constantly changes as human attempt to understand the secrets of the creation. For me the search for knowledge glorifies God, and reveals the hand of God in its marvelous design. Some use science to deny God. They are just as rigid as the people who have faith in God they condemn as foolish. It is horrifying how people use their beliefs to control others and make their views exclude others from their world. Religion is too often primitive tribalism. The world is divided between them and us. My understanding of Jesus is completely the opposite way of seeing other people. I could give you numerous examples in the Gospels of Jesus responding lovingly to people who were considered enemies by the Jewish people. Jesus loved Samaritans, Roman soldiers, prostitutes, lepers, demoniacs, and idol worshippers. Jesus did not come into the world to condemn the world, but to save us from sin and death. My Jesus includes the whole diversity of humanity. We are all sinners and all of us are on our own spiritual journey."

"Are you saying," Dan interrupted, "all religions are the same?"

"Absolutely not," Mark answered. "Jesus Christ is the perfect revelation of God and that makes Christianity the way, the truth, and the life. We should respect all religions, but we have the means to know God intimately in a relationship with Jesus. As Christians we know God as one being in three persons who reaches out to humankind in love. This is part of the unique understanding of our faith. We believe in God who loves us and asks us to return that love and to love each other. Christianity is different from other religions, and there are many more differences. I believe it is contrary to the nature of God for people to use fear or coercion to make people agree with us."

Dan realized Mark had needed to explain himself and had prepared these comments. What Mark said made sense to him. He reflected on his own experience of God. As someone who had turned away from God for most of his adult life, God was ready to accept him the moment he asked for help. Maybe he was not the biggest sinner in the world, but God accepted him when he asked. That was the Jesus he knew. This conversation with Mark confirmed his love for Jesus. The more he knew about Jesus and the Christian faith the deeper he loved it.

After this conversation with Mark, Dan was more prepared to appreciate the whole range of Christian traditions and practices. He came to admire Pastor Andy for his inclusive spirit. He went to Susan to talk about their honeymoon plans and the wideness of God's mercy. Susan was delighted with the possibility of a honeymoon on the beach in Belize, and she already knew the extravagant love of God long before Dan. The wedding plans were being finalized. Everything was going so beautifully for her and Dan.

Chapter 14 - The Best of Times

Dan began researching Belize on the internet in preparation for the honeymoon trip. Susan was taking care of the wedding plans. Life was good. They felt an exhilarating spirit that comes when planning something so hopeful as marriage. Everyone was happy for them, expect one person. Jay was furious. He had trouble concealing his rage. He perceived the marriage of his ex-wife as a loss of his children and the loss of a wife he owned. He did acknowledge the divorce as legitimate. He was convinced it was only further proof of personal satanic attack. In his mind he had to stop the marriage at any cost.

Pastor Andy invited Dan and Susan to participate in pre-marriage counseling which was customary policy at the church. Technically speaking marriage, is not a sacrament in the protestant church, but Pastor Andy felt it was a holy sacrament. He wanted to share his understanding with every couple he had the privilege to counsel before performing the wedding service. Susan and Dan understood much about the joys and tears of being married, but they learned in the sessions with pastor Andy the theology of Christian marriage and how that was expressed in the wedding service. Pastor Andy explained to them the option of celebrating Holy Communion as part of the service. They readily agreed to share this with their church family who would be attending the wedding. They found a harpist who would play some special instrumental music during the service. Susan contacted a friend who owned a flower shop to do the floral arrangements. She knew a store that sold wedding dresses at a fraction of the original cost and found the perfect dress. Dan designed the wedding invitations and had them printed on hand-made paper. The wedding reception was the only unresolved part they struggled with.

Originally Dan wanted to have the reception at the most expensive restaurant in town. Susan was opposed to this extravagance expense. She advocated they have the reception in the basement of the church and just serve appetizers. Dan knew that the church would not allow alcohol to be served and he wanted a big party with a meal and a band for dancing. Susan was hesitant to accept Dan's need for a big party. Eventually she recognized this was important to him and agreed if he could find a place that was not so pricey. After much research Dan found a park on the Ohio River that could be rented which included a beautiful house and outdoor shelter at a reasonable cost. Then he and Susan began investigating caterers. After considering numerous menus, they both thought about the Chinese restaurant were Dan had proposed marriage. Dan contacted Mrs. Wong and she enthusiastically agreed to provide the meal for two hundred people. They found a service that would set up a bar. Through a friend they contacted a band that played danceable music. Everything was coming together for the wedding.

Troy and Dianna were excited about the marriage. They knew that their mother was happier than she had been in many years. They liked Dan and felt comfortable about moving into his house. Dan had not tried to be a father figure to them. He was uncertain about becoming a step father and was taking his relationship with his new family slowly. He wanted Troy and Dianna to know him and like him. He thought it best to support their mother and just be himself. They had asked Dianna to be one of the bridesmaids in the wedding party, and she was happy to be included. Troy was asked to be an usher and to light the candles at the beginning of the service. They were planning on three pairs of candelabras in addition to the altar candles so this was a big job. Dianna was very pleased with the dress they bought for her and the fancy hair style that was going to be done on the morning of the wedding. When Troy and Dianna had their infrequent visits with their father they avoided any mention of the wedding because they knew it upset him. When he asked them questions about Dan, they were as evasive as possible. They were painfully aware of their father's contempt for Dan.

The weeks passed quickly and the families began to make plans for consolidating two households into one. Dan had plenty of room in his house so each of the children would have their own bedroom. Dan's house was still sparsely furnished so he had very little to move to make room for his new family. The problem was what of Susan's furniture they should keep and what to get rid of. Most of her furniture was second hand when she got it decades earlier and was not worth keeping. There were some family treasure and sentimental pieces that were important to retain. Then there were all those myriad items of yard tools, cleaning supplies, storage containers in the attic and basement, and accumulated stuff from years of living. Dan knew it would sort itself out over time. Susan was not as confident as Dan.

On Saturdays Dan and Susan spent the morning working at the soup kitchen. Troy and Dianna joined them when they did not have other activities. Troy had soccer practice this particular Saturday and Dianna had figure skating practice. The soup kitchen preparation was busy because they had two dozen volunteers helping prepare the meals. At quarter past eleven as they were loading the van with the food to take it to where it would be served, there was an urgent phone call for Susan. Dan overheard the message and was alarmed and followed her to the phone. He saw Susan's face go pale as she listened to the caller. She kept saying, 'We'll be right there!"

When she got off the phone she told Dan her house was on fire. There had been an explosion and the fire men were already there. One neighbor called another neighbor who knew where they were. They rushed to the car and raced home. The street to their house was closed by the police so they had to park over a block away and run through the police barricade to Susan's house. By this time most of the flames had been extinguished by the firemen. Gigantic clouds of gray and black smoke were pouring out of every window. There were at least five different crews of firemen shootings gallons of water into the windows of the house. Water was flooding out the front door, onto the steps, and cascading down the front walk into the street. There was nothing Susan and Dan could do but watch as the firemen saturated the house with water. After a half an hour the smoke was almost gone and some of the fire crew were retracting their hoses. Dan looked around for the fire chief and found him talking to the police. Dan approached the fire chief and asked to talk with him. The fire chief wanted to question him as well. He asked if they had smelled gas anytime in the house and particularly in the basement. Dan replied he didn't think so. The fire chief said they were going to do an investigation because the fire had apparently started with an explosion from a gas leak in the basement. The neighbors told him there had been a loud explosion around ten forty-five and then flames burst out of the basement windows. Then the fire chief asked if anyone had smelled gas at any time in the last week. Dan said he would speak to the kids when they came home.

Dan went to Susan and asked her about smelling gas. She was certain there was no gas odor when she had started some laundry early that morning in the basement. "Why do they want to know?" she asked. Dan told her the neighbors reported an explosion and immediately flame came out from the basement. Dan said they were fortunate the neighbors called the fire department as fast as they did because the house could have burned to the ground. Then it occurred to him if anyone had been home they might have been killed. Then a frightening thought occurred to Dan. Without thinking he said to Susan, "Thank God nobody was home or they could have been killed." Susan burst into tears.

As the firemen began to withdraw, a few firemen explored the inside of the house. They told Dan and Susan they needed to stay out of the house for a few days until it was determined if it was structurally safe for them to enter. The fireman told them to contact the insurance agent immediately and to keep everyone out of the house. The windows, which were all broken, needed to be covered with plywood and the front and back door padlocked as soon as possible. Susan asked about her things.

One fireman said, "Lady, everything in the house that was either burned, or ruined by smoke, and soaked in water. I hope you got good insurance because there is nothing in there you want to keep."

Dan followed the fireman to the fire truck and asked, "How do you know how it started?"

"We see this sort of thing all the time," the fireman said. "It was a gas explosion in the basement. Too bad you didn't notice the gas leak before this happened. It was leaking pretty strong to blow this bad. You should have smelled it."

"What caused it to ignite?" Dan asked.

"Anything will set it off," the fireman explained. "The thermostat started the furnace, or an appliance kicked on. Any spark will get it going. You're just lucky nobody was home when it happened. Someone should have smelled the gas."

Dan was getting annoyed with the comments about smelling the gas. He asked Susan about an odor in the basement again, and again she said there was no odor. Dan was troubled by the mysterious, sudden gas leak that has destroyed her house.

Susan was concerned with the kids and their loss of clothes. Dan said he would buy them clothes. That was not a problem. He told Susan they would be staying at his house tonight and everything would be okay. Susan held on to Dan for awhile as they stared in silence at the sad smoke stained house. After a long silence Susan said, "I guess we'll have to put off the wedding."

"No way!" Dan responded, "We're getting married as planned. Nothing is going to change that. We're getting you a new wedding dress and new clothes. We're going ahead with the wedding as planned."

"I don't know if I can," Susan murmured. "I just don't know."

"We're going to move past this and, with the help of God, things will all work out for the best. Remember what you always say, "All things work for God's good purpose for those who love God." We're going to believe that, and go on with our life. Are you willing to trust God will help us work our way through this?"

"I want to believe you," Susan replied. "I hope God will give me the strength, this is so hard right now. I want to believe. God help me!"

Off in the distance Susan saw Troy and Dianna arguing with the police. She called to them and the police let them through. Susan dried her face with her sleeve. Troy and Diana rushed into her arms weeping. She consoled them and told them everything would turn out fine. She was a pillar of strength to her children. They were devastated. Susan told her children, "We're leaving all that old junk behind and we're moving into Dan's house today. And we're all going shopping this afternoon for new clothes. And we're starting our life brand new. Starting now we have a new beginning. I was tired of all that old stuff and I'm glad to be rid of it. Who wants to go shopping?" Troy and Dianna were amazed at their mother's strength. Dan thanked God.

As they were leaving the house the police were wrapping the house with warning tape. It read "keep out by police order."

They went to a department store and bought lots of clothes for Susan, Troy and Dianna. They had a late lunch nearby and returned to Dan's house. Mindy was happy to greet everyone into her home. Now Mindy had a boy and girl to play with all the time. Susan and Dianna took Dan's room. Troy slept on an air mattress in his room and Dan slept on the sofa. They watched movies on TV and ordered pizza for supper. No one had home work because it was all lost in their old house. Sunday morning they went to church and were embarrassed by the concerns and questions from their church family.

After church they went by the old house. Dan opened the garage and backed out Susan's car which was untouched by the fire. Susan and the kids took it to a car wash to try and get the smoke odor out of the car. Dan went into the house through the door from the garage into the kitchen. On the main floor everything was soaking wet and the walls and ceilings were stained gray with smoke stain. Dan ventured down the basement stairs. By this time most of the water had drained out through the floor drains. The basement was blackened. Only the skeletons of the furniture remained. There was nothing to recover from the basement. When he got close to the furnace he noticed the gas line to the furnace was disconnected, and there was a pipe wrench lying on the floor nearby. He got out of there as fast as possible. He looked down the stairs to see if his wet shoes had left footprints. The stairs were so saturate with water his wet shoes left no trace. He got out of the house and called the fire department. Because it was Sunday, the fire chief was not on duty. He inquired when they would do the investigation into the fire. They assured him it would be first thing Monday. Dan knew that gas line didn't come apart by itself.

He didn't say anything to Susan because he wanted to hear what the fire investigators had to say. Monday morning he was at Susan's house early waiting to meet the firemen. One of the neighbors came by and offered his condolences about the accident. When the neighbor was leaving he asked Dan if he had to talked to Jay. Dan said he hadn't seen him.

The neighbor said, "Oh, too bad, you must just missed him. Over a spell he was here."

"Did you talk to him?" Dan asked.

"Not much," He replied, "Just told him how real sorry I was about his nice house. You know he don't live here no more. Recon family troubles, don't you know. Well, I'll be seeing y'all."

Dan waited for the firemen. They arrived about nine o'clock and spent an hour in the house. When they came out, Dan asked them if they found anything. They said it was a fire of suspicious origin. "Oh yeah!" Dan exclaimed. "Why did you conclude that?"

"The gas line to the furnace was disconnected," the fireman answered.

"Could the fire could have done that?" Dan asked.

The firemen looked at him like he was crazy, and they all shook their heads. Then one of the firemen looked Dan in the eye and said, "They would have had to smell gas in the basement."

"Of course, they would have smelled gas," Dan shot back, "if they had been home when someone took that pipe apart."

Suddenly he was surrounded by the firemen. They demanded to know what he was holding back. He told them he couldn't prove anything, but he added, "When they left the house at eight AM there was no gas leak. The neighbors said the house blew up about an hour and a half later. This was no slow leak. It was a major leak. Someone must have got into the house Saturday morning and uncoupled that pipe." He was careful to not mention the pipe wrench because he didn't want to reveal he had been in the house against orders. He knew they had seen the wrench. They had to have noticed it. They wanted to know if he knew who might have done it. He told them he suspected the ex-husband. They asked him for proof and he told them he had none. They walked away.

That afternoon the police stopped by Dan's house and asked him the same questions. He gave them the same answers. He felt like he was now a suspect because he was accusing someone of arson with no evidence. Unless someone saw Jay enter the house on Saturday morning there was no proof he had anything to do with the fire. He also questioned in his own mind whether Jay was capable of such an act.

Over the next few days Dan, Susan, Troy, and Dianna shopped and got clothes and furniture for their new life together. Eventually they got permission to enter Susan's old house and salvaged a few things that were worth saving. It was surprising how easy it was to lose everything and replace most of it and start anew. The police investigation came to no conclusion other than "a fire of suspicious origin." Everyday Dan and Susan thanked God in their prayers no one was hurt in the fire. After a week or so, the shock began to wear off so they were able to give their attention to the wedding preparations.

Chapter 15 - The Big Event

"Marriage is the highest calling," Pastor Andy told Dan and Susan, "and this is what we will be celebrating at your wedding." As the three of them discussed the marriage vows at length, each person in their own way realized how these vows stated simply what they wanted in marriage, and hoped it would always be true for their partners. Dan and Susan were also painfully reminded of how their marriages had failed. Somehow those vows had been forgotten. They were confident this time they were not going to make the same mistakes they had made in the past, but they were aware that people change over time and they had no control over that. When a person changes so much that the partnership is no longer viable, the marriage is doomed. They talked about how there was a time not too long ago when married people who lost interest in each other just tolerated a cessation of overt hostilities because divorce was so unacceptable. Today, when one partner is unhappy for any reason they head for divorce court without much hesitation. Dan and Susan discussed these things openly with Pastor Andy were committed to make their marriage work.

Some of Susan's friends had asked Susan if they could decorate the church sanctuary for the wedding. It would be their gift to her and Dan. Susan was delighted to be relieved of the responsibility for decorating the sanctuary and left the details to her friends. When she arrived at the church two hours before the service, her friends were just finishing the surprise they had planned for her and Dan. This was the most extravagant decoration of Hartwell Church anyone had ever attempted. They had used a connection with a florist to purchase flowers from the wholesale distributor. They had bought cartons of white carnations, daisies, and baby's breath ferns. On every window sill, steps up to the cancel, and woven into a rented trellis were bouquets of flowers. There were hundreds of simple arrangements strategically placed everywhere. Susan's friends had placed three pairs of standing candelabras in the front of the sanctuary. One pair was in front the chancel, one pair beside the communion table, and one pair behind the communion table. They were shaped at an angle so that it formed a two sides of a triangle which pointed toward the cross that hung on the back wall of the sanctuary. There were candles in brass holders on end of every other pew. Flowers were tied by white ribbons around each one of them. The communion table had an exquisite arrangement of every type of white flower contributed by Susan's friend who was a professional flower arranger. The effect of simple white flower arrangements everywhere was breathtaking. Susan was overwhelmed when she saw how beautiful the church looked.

When Dan came into the sanctuary he was so nervous he didn't notice any of the decorations until they were pointed out to him. When he looked around, he was speechless. He could only think how much love was displayed by their church friends in this extravagant display. He arrived just in time to help the harpist wheel her enormous instrument through the big double doors at the front of the church building. The harpist quickly unpacked her harp and began tuning the instrument. Soon the wedding party was assembled in two separate groups on different sides of the building. The groomsmen kept Dan away from Susan and had never seen her in her wedding dress. A few minutes before the wedding was scheduled to begin, Dan, the best man Peter, the groomsmen, and the pastor proceeded to the front of the sanctuary and up on to the chancel steps. There they waited in front of the large gathering of friends and family for the procession of the bridesmaids.

After the bridesmaids and maid of honor were escorted into their positions, the harpist concluded her music. The organist then began playing the traditional "Here Comes the Bride." Susan entered the back of the sanctuary and slowly came down the center aisle on the arm of her father. Dan was spellbound. Susan looked so beautiful. Her hair was piled up on her head in a fashion he had never seen her wear before. She had more make-up on then he was accustomed to seeing. The dress was simple but elegant. (Fortunately the dress was being altered at the wedding dress shop when the fire destroyed Susan's house.) Dan stood frozen by Susan's radiant loveliness. Pastor Andy leaned over an whispered in Dan's ear to descend the three steps to receive his bride. He was given her arm by her father Tom, and helped her negotiate the steps up the chancel cautiously watching the hem of the floor length dress. They stood before Pastor Andy and he smiled broadly to them. This helped them relax a little.

Although the wedding service took twenty-five minutes, to Dan and Susan they were the shortest minutes of their life. It was almost over too soon when Dan was invited to kiss the bride. Kissing Susan in front of all those people suddenly embarrassed Dan, and tried to give her a modest peck on the lips. She was not going to let him get away with such a modest kiss and she pulled him close and kissed him hard and long. There was a quiet giggle that ran through the congregation. "Friends I present to you," Pastor Andy announced, "Dan and Susan Cooper!" The guests applauded and stood as the newly married couple started up the center-aisle.

During the wedding Mark and Peter had been nervously keeping an eye out for Jay to appear. They were concerned he would disrupt the wedding. They were greatly relieved he never showed up.

After the guests left the church building for the reception hall down by the Ohio River, the wedding party and relatives posed for pictures. Fortunately this only took an hour so they got to the reception before the waiting guests were too bored. When they arrived at the reception there was a wonderful Chinese dinner prepared for them. Everyone complimented Dan and Susan on how lovely the sanctuary was decorated and how beautiful Susan looked. It was not just the hairdo, make-up, or dress that made her so gorgeous. The fact that she was so happy radiated joy that was beyond description. Every man in the room who danced with her took the opportunity to kiss her. A few men were a bit overly enthusiastic, but Dan restrained his jealousy. Susan enjoyed the attention.

That night they stayed at a very posh hotel in the honeymoon suite and consummated their love for each other. The next morning they managed to get going before noon and went home to be with the kids. Troy and Dianna had had a wonderful time at the wedding reception and had only gotten to bed after two in the morning. Susan's sister Beth had stayed with them and she was going to stay at Dan and Susan's house while they were off on their honeymoon.

While they were busy packing for their trip to tropical Belize Dan got an unexpected call from a high-end furniture chain in California. They expressed interest in looking at examples of a style of furniture that would be suitable for their California lifestyle clientele. Dan had done some small sales with this company, but had never had a big order from them. He explained that he had just gotten married and was leaving for his honeymoon that night. He told them he would be in contact with them as soon as he got back. He hoped he had not lost this opportunity but he really didn't have time to organize a presentation for them to meet their expectations. He knew this California furniture company was quite capable of placing a million dollar order. A large order from this company could be the biggest thing that ever happened to his business. He just had to put it out of his mind and give Susan his undivided attention.

The flight to Belize began with a flight to Houston, Texas. The plane from Cincinnati airport left at six am which meant they were supposed to be at the airport at four am because it was the beginning of an international flight. Even though they got up at three am and had their bags packed, it was difficult saying goodbye to the children and making sure they had not forgotten anything. They got to the ticket gate just before five am and there was a long line of tired and anxious passengers ahead of them. When they finally got to the ticket counter, received their tickets, and checked their large bags they raced to security with their carry-ons. Susan had forgotten about the restrictions on liquids and had all of her shampoos, lotions, deodorant, toothpaste, and other essentials confiscated by security. She was beside herself. Dan reassured her they could replace everything in Belize. She had doubts she would be able to duplicate what had been taken. They got to the gate just as the plane was boarding.

The flight to Houston was uneventful. Susan slept through the flight, and Dan read an inspirational book about Jesus. He resisted the temptation to wake Susan to share the insights the author had about faith. When they arrived in Houston they called home and talked to Troy and Dianna. They had enough of a layover to get breakfast and were at the gate for the flight to Belize with time to spare. As they waited in the boarding area, they were surprised by two groups of Christians all identified by their brightly colored tee shirts who were going to Belize on mission trips. Dan became engaged in a conversation with one of the missionaries. According to the missionary, who identified himself as Harry from Coldwater, Iowa, this was his eighth mission trip to Belize in four years. They emphasized medical work but also helped built schools, churches, and homes. "They had two medical teams," explained Harry, "The surgical team works at the hospital, and another team that visits a different village every day, and examined about two hundred people at each village. We are taking dozens of suitcases of medicine to distribute." They invited Dan and Susan to come by where they were staying and they could see the work the missionaries were doing. Dan got an address and phone number on how to contact them in Belize. Dan did not know how far it was from where they were staying in Hopkins to where they were working in Orange Walk. He and Susan talked about it and agreed that it would be interesting to see what they were doing.

On the two-and-one-half hour flight to Belize, Dan read more about the importance of having a personnel relationship with Jesus and not letting religion get in the way of that intimacy. As he read, he was intrigued by the missionaries who dominated the flight. They were constantly visiting each other, exchanging seats, and full of excitement. One of them noticed the book he was reading and complimented Dan on his choice of author. Dan wondered how he was going to know Jesus on a honeymoon in the tropics. He wondered if this was contradictory to mix pleasure with faith.

When they landed in Belize there was a long line at immigration. They waited quite a while for the baggage to arrive on the carousel. Then lining up at customs to check luggage. The missionaries where having trouble with customs getting the dozens of suitcases full of medicine cleared. They were inspecting the contents of the bags and checking them against lists to make sure everything was in order. Finally, Dan and Susan got cleared and found the car rental agency where they had reserved their Land Cruiser. Susan asked when they could get to a store to replace the items she had surrendered at security. Dan had no idea, but assured her they would find a place. The agent at the car rental overheard them, and told them about a big market on the way out of town. As they went outside to inspect the rental vehicle for damage before they left the airport, they ran into the mission group leader inspecting one of the many vans they had rented. He mentioned again that they were invited to visit them and see what they were doing. He told them the local people they worked with were some of the finest people he had ever met. Dan and Susan would be welcome to eat with them, and if they needed a place to stay overnight, that could be easily arranged. He hoped they would seriously consider the offer because they loved to share how God was blessing their work. "You know," said Harry, "this might even be something your church back in Kentucky might be interested in

Dan told him that their church was very mission oriented and it might well be an opportunity to expand their mission work. Dan asked if he knew the store that the rental agent had mentioned. The missionary said he knew it and they would have everything Dan and Susan needed. He told them it was a good place to stock up on supplies for their vacation.

When they left the airport they soon found the big, modern market they were looking for. In addition to replacing everything Susan had lost at airport security, they found all kinds of things they would use over the next days in Belize. They bought snacks, sodas, swimming masks, snorkels, fins, flashlights, batteries, an underwater cameras, and gaudy beach towels. They had fun shopping for their adventure. Off they went following the map headed for the three hour drive to Hopkins.

Chapter 16 - Belize it or not

The scenery of the drive west and south through the country side and mountains of central Belize was beautiful. After they left the Western highway they were traveling in the foothills of Maya Mountains. The mountains are covered in lush tropical vegetation and the two lane road called the Hummingbird Highway is like a roller coaster. Dan soon became aware of the importance of paying attention to his gas gauge because of the lack of gasoline stations along the way. They made one unscheduled stop at Blue Hole waterfall somewhere west of Belmopan on the Hummingbird Highway. This was a enchanted landscape where the steep path leads through the forest to a majestic waterfall. Children were wading and swimming in the water. Dan and Susan were tempted to join the children in the refreshing water but didn't have their swimsuits readily available and decided against opening their suitcases. This spot in the mountains looked like paradise out in the middle of nowhere.

The turn off for Hopkins was not well marked and they almost missed it. Since the road surface immediately became dirt and rough they started to question if they had made a mistake, but they sensed the ocean was directly ahead of them so they continued on. When they arrived in Hopkins they saw a little store on their left, and a bar and restaurant on the right, so they were relieved they were on the right road. After a couple of miles heading north away from the village, they followed the hand-painted sign that took them on the one lane road to Coconut Cabanas. Just as they approached the ocean, there was a cluster of small wooden buildings on tall stilts scattered on the edge of the beach where the palm trees grew. They parked the car and went searching for anyone who could tell them if this was where they had reservations. In one of the buildings they found a group of women practicing yoga. The leader of the class was in her eighties and in terrific physical condition. She stopped the class and walked over to Dan and Susan. "Hello," she said in her soft staccato, "my name is Billie and you must be Frank and

Susan from the United States. Welcome to the nuts of Coconuts Cabanas."

"Yes, my name is Dan, and this is Susan and we just arrived in Belize."

"Dan. Oh yes. Dan. That's it! You're Dan and Susan, and we have been expecting you. Let me show you your cabana. Have you eaten? Will you want dinner here tonight or do you have other plans? I think Hilda got enough fish at the market for all of us. Do you eat fish? Should I tell Hilda you'll be having dinner with us then?"

As they walked to the cabana closest to the ocean, Dan replied. "Yes, dinner would be wonderful. We have only had snacks all day. So this is our house?"

Billy climbed up the long flight of stairs to the deck on the front of the house and opened the unlocked door and invited them in. The cabana was one large room with a table and chairs, a double bed, and, built into a corner of the room, was a bathroom. They were delighted to know there was a modern flush toilet, shower, and hot water. The house had been made by a Mennonite crew of carpenters and was made mostly of mahogany and Santa Maria wood. The ceiling was open to exposed rafters and made the building feel very spacious. There were three ceiling fans, and the walls were almost all windows with screens. The windows had horizontal wooden louvers that allowed the maximum amount of ocean breeze into the room. Billie explained, "You won't need any air conditioning because there is always a beautiful breeze from the ocean in the evening. You can move right in. When I find Kenny he will bring them the key. I don't know if Kenny is back from Dangriga yet. He had gone to get some light bulbs and paper towels. I don't know what he does in Dangriga. He always takes so long on these simple errands. He is getting forgetful in his advanced years." Off she went back to her yoga class.

Dan and Susan collapsed on the bed laughing.

"What do you think?" Dan asked Susan holding her hands in his.

"I love it," she answered. "Do you like it?"

"It's perfect," he replied. Let's go get our stuff. I want my bathing suit because I'm going for a swim. Want to join me?"

They raced to the car and hauled their suitcases across the sand, up the stairs, and into the cabana. In no time they were changed into bathing suits and racing for the water. Their cabana was about thirty feet from the ocean. The turquoise blue water was crystal clear and the perfect temperature. Running as fast as they could, they and dove into the surf. They played and swam in the rolling waves until they were exhausted. Susan tried to push Dan under the water but he evaded her grip. He then grabbed hold of her legs and flipped her backwards. They spread their new tropical patterned brightly colored beach towels on the sand and soon fell asleep since they had been up since three am.

They had not been sleeping long when they were awoken by a very tall stately looking older man standing over them.

"Your key, sir," he said. " If you need another key I might be able to come up with one.I hope you have sun tan lotion on because that sun will burn you up sleeping on the beach!"

Dan and Susan suddenly realized they had forgotten to put on sun block. They introduced themselves to the gentleman and thanked him for the key.

"Oh, yes. Quite so!" he responded. "I'm Kenny, the proprietor of this fine establishment . You have already met my lovely bride, Billie. She helps out around the place with odds and ends form time to time. If there is anything you need, just ask me. Billie is getting so forgetful these days. She has a good heart, you see. Do you want to attend her yoga classes? She would love to have you. Don't forget dinner is at six sharp, and we don't wait for anyone. The bar is open anytime. Ask Hilda for anything. Oh, you'll meet Hilda at dinner. Just help yourself if we're not around. You can tell me what you had and I'll put it on your tab.

Is that okay with you?" Kenny paused for a moment before adding, "We're not too formal around here."

"We're delighted with the accommodations," Dan responded.

Kenny turned away and strutted off across the beach.

Susan went back to their cabana and retrieved the sun block lotion. Susan said to Dan, "Good thing Kenny awakened us when he did. If we had slept for an hour or two in the afternoon sun we would have been badly burned. Sun poisoning is a miserable experience."

That's why Kenny awakened them when he found them sleeping on the beach. After Dan and Susan covered their white skin with great globs of lotion they resumed their nap on the beach. When they awoke their skin was glistening with tiny beads of sweat from cooking in the tropical sun. " Let's cool off in the water," Dan suggested.

"What a brilliant idea," Susan replied.

Dan was getting very aroused looking at Susan in her bathing suit jumping around in the water. He tried to engage her in the ocean in some serious petting. She eventually pushed him away and teasingly said, "You'll have to wait 'til tonight." They went back to the towels on the beach to dry off before getting ready for dinner.

As they were lying there, Dan turned to Susan and said, "Is it legal to be this happy?"

"Are you kidding?" Susan asked Dan. "Don't you think God wants his children to be happy? Didn't Jesus say, 'May my joy be in you, and may your joy be complete'?"

"Thank you for that scripture," Dan responded. "Sometimes I have trouble accepting the fact that God wants us to be happy. You know it's true what Mark said after we went to Jay's church, 'Some Christians act like they were baptized in vinegar.'" Susan giggled. "Do you think Jesus was happy, or was he always so serious like you see him in the paintings of him?"

"My favorite picture of Jesus is of him laughing," Susan answered. "Some biblical scholars have written that we miss the humor in many of Jesus' sayings. He often used hyperbole to both make a point and to catch the attention of his disciples with humor. Everywhere he went he attracted great crowds. Of course, some of those people came for healing, some came to listen to his teaching, and still others came out of curiosity. But I am convinced many came because he drew them to him. He must have made people laugh. If he had been gloomy and anxious, he never would have drawn those crowds. I believe he was wonderful to be around, and people smiled around him. I think he radiated joy and peace. That's the Jesus I know."

Dan lay his head down on the sand and looked up at the blue sky. He closed his eyes and tried to imagine Jesus the way Susan described him. This combined perfectly with the ineffable experience of love he had had over a year before. He knew that Jesus knew everything he thought and did. He was painfully aware that he was accountable for both his thoughts and deeds, but this was bearable because he was certain that his sins were forgiven. Dan knew Jesus had died on the cross for that very reason. When Dan did something he regretted, he asked for forgiveness and that was the end of it. He tried with all his might to not repeat the mistakes he made.

Lying next to this adorable woman who had given herself in marriage to him, he was now able to focus his desire for her and put away the sin of lust that had been bothering him for quite a while. In his support group they had often discussed lust. Every man he knew struggled with this desire. They had come to the conclusion that lust was excessive sexual desire and definitely something more than finding women attractive. Now that he could express his desire appropriately, he was certain that he had conquered the lust issue. Dan smiled as he remembered thinking on the plane to Belize if 'the pleasures of the honeymoon on the beach in the tropics' was going to alienate him from God. He realized God cared about his happiness. He was happier than he could ever remember, and he was feeling a greater closeness with God than ever before.

Soon it was time for Dan and Susan to get ready for dinner. After showering and dressing they went to search for the building where dinner was served. This turned out to be the only building not on tall stilts. They went inside and were greeted by Billy and Kenny. They sat at the table which was set for six people and Hilda began serving the meal. The fish was red snapper, fresh caught the day before. It was served with the head and tail intact. Susan was not accustomed to having the whole fish on a plate. She followed the lead of the others and began to enjoy the fish. While they were eating another couple showed up for dinner and made their apologies. Hilda brought their food. They didn't talk much.

Dan asked Kenny how they had come to own a resort in Belize, and Billy and Kenny told their whole story. Kenny said, "We had a little money when we retired and wanted to invest in a business that would provide some income, and give us a great life."

"Don't forget about the cold Canadian winters part of the story," Billie interjected. "That is important you now."

"Of course," Kenny added. "I was just coming to that bit of the story. We just about had it with the snow and ice. So we investigated Belize and after two years of searching we found this plot of land. That was back in nineteen---."

"Nineteen eighty-nine," Billie remarked, "How can you forget the year we bought this land. There was just a shack. No water or electric. Just our little shack on the beach is all it was then."

"And look at us now," Kenny interrupted. We were pioneer. We were some of the first whites to live in Hopkins. Every one wondered about us then. But we showed them a thing or two. Ain't that so, old girl?"

"What a fascinating story," Dan said. He admire them for being so adventurous. They clearly loved life and were devoted to each other over sixty years of marriage.

During dinner Dan bought a bottle of wine from the bar to share around the table. It didn't last very long among six people. Kenny said, "You should go to the center of town to hear the drumming. We highly recommended it. The Garifuni have been doing this drumming all the way from Africa. It's quite stirring."

"Hopkins was one of the few places of Garifuni culture," Billie added. "These people were Africans who had been brought to the Caribbean to be slaves. God love them. They rebelled and established their own communities. They were eventually forced to relocate and many had settled in Belize. They had their own African language and customs. There is nothing like it!"

That evening Dan and Susan had a magical time listening to the drumming. They bought a couple of cold Belikin beers at the bar. The drumming lasted for hours. Some of the women danced to the drums. This was pure rhythm that sets the heart racing. The tempo increased as the night went on. More drummers joined the group. Dan and Susan were dizzy with the frenzy of the drums.

When they returned to their little cabana on the Caribbean Sea they were happy to stare at the beautiful stars for a short while from their little porch. The Milky Way was plainly visible as a blur of stars running across the sky. They saw several shooting stars. After an hour watching the heavens they went to bed.

They slept a deep sleep for ten hours. The bright Caribbean sun streaming through the windows woke them. They had told Hilda at dinner they would like to have breakfast. She made them a huge breakfast of waffles, scrambled eggs, and bacon. They thanked Hilda for the delicious breakfast. They went to the beach on full stomachs. That afternoon they made arrangements with Kenny for a local guide to pick them up at the beach in front of their cabana, to take them snorkeling out on the coral reef that Belize is famous for around the world.

They saw a world of fantastic shapes and colors completely different from the world above the water. They saw so many strange fish and creatures going about their business oblivious to the two intruders in their world. The plants were waving in the ebb and flow of the underwater currents. After a couple of hours of snorkeling the reef Dan and Susan talked about the unbelievable diversity and beauty of God's creation hidden in the ocean. They had never seen anything like it. Documentaries about underwater adventures didn't compare to the actual experience of swimming in a coral reef. When they returned to Coconut Cabanas they were exhausted and had a much needed nap before dinner.

That night at dinner they asked Kenny about visiting some Mayan ruins. He told them about Xunantunich just outside of San Ignacio, which was a few hours drive from Hopkins. They decided they would make a daytrip to see the Mayan ruins the next day. During the conversation over dinner, Kenny inquired about Dan's occupation. When Dan told him about being in the furniture business, Kenny was eager for him to visit a Mennonite furniture maker in Shipyard. He explained it was on the way to San Ignacio and he would give him directions to Wilhelm Peters factory in Shipyard. Dan looked at Susan to see how she was responding to the suggestion and she nodded her approval. They added the furniture factory to their itinerary for the next day.

The next morning they were up at sunrise and had a modest breakfast to get an early start. After a couple hours they found the road north to Shipyard and followed Kenny's directions. They realized there were no road signs and they had to carefully follow the directions. Dan had spotted Peter's factory long before they saw the sign because of all the wood stacked in huge meticulous arrays surrounding a complex of white metal barns. There was no showroom. In a storage building where the finished product was stacked for shipment was a wide variety of furniture. All the furniture had natural finishes to show the beauty of the mahogany it was made from. The workmanship was similar to the Amish furniture that Dan admired so much which was made in the Ohio. Immediately Dan knew he was onto something. He asked if he could take photographs of the furniture. The man he asked looked at him blankly and walked away. Soon an older man appeared. He was the owner of the business, Mr. Wilhelm Peters. He was one of the few people there who spoke English. Dan explained who he was and why he wanted to take pictures.

Mr. Peters said, "Yah, sure. You take picture and we make some business together. I sell for you at good dollars if you do much business. Jacob, you commin' zee hear now and clean up deese good for the pictures."

Dan went crazy taking pictures of everything. He was thinking how this had the look of the contemporary California market. Jacob moved and wiped every item so Dan could get great photos. Dan was so excited he wasn't thinking of cost or shipping yet. He knew his import business and he would figure out those issues after he got good images. After he had shot everything he could find he started asking the price of different items. He kept copious notes of what Mr. Peters quoted. Then Dan knew he had found what he was looking for at a cost that made it practical to ship to the United States and sell wholesale. Then he asked Mr. Peters if he was capable of filling some really big orders and packing them in containers and sending them to the port in Belize City. "Yah," Mr. Peters said. "We have too many containers in Shipyard. Our imports all come in dem big containers. My brother Heinrich has two dozen containers behind his store and he has a truck for to move them whenever da vant. You send me order on my internet and I give you bank account where youse transfer the dollars from the US bank to me. I make what you vant in one month. My brother, Friedrich, got big factory in Shipyard too, you know. He help make furniture for me too, you know. How much you vant now?"

"Not today," Dan mused. "When we go back to the US in a week, I will contact my sources and show them the photos I took today. I am sure they will be interested and then I will place an order. This is exactly what we have been looking for. This is going to be really big, Mr. Peters. Give me your card so we can keep in touch."

"Maybe you vant to be looking some of the other things we make in dis next building now?" Mr. Peters asked.

Dan looked at Susan and Susan looked back at Dan in amazement. They walked to the next building. Inside was the really special furniture. The first piece they encountered was a table made of bloodwood which were naturally brilliant red. They saw chairs, cabinets, bureaus, desks, bed frames, benches, shelves, and mirror frames made from all types of exotic hardwoods. Mr. Peters identified which were made from purple heart, zericote, rosewood, iron wood, tempisque, cristobal, mahogany, and baca. There were woods Dan had never seen before. He started taking more pictures. Mr. Peters sent Jacob to get little samples of some of the different woods. Jacob wrote the names of the wood on the samples. Dan shot hundreds of pictures on his digital camera. When they left the factory Dan was so excited he was like a child.

After lunch in a restaurant in San Ignacio they headed for the Mayan ruins. The afternoon walking around the magnificent ruins of Xunantinich was amazing. They were blessed with a very knowledgeable Mayan guide who explained the buildings to them and aspects of Mayan culture. The magnificent structures of Mayan civilization were most impressive to Dan and Susan. The whole time Dan was distracted, thinking about the furniture he had seen and how well it was going to sell in California. When they arrived back in Hopkins that night, Dan could hardly sleep because he was so excited about the find he had made that day. Susan suggested they go into Hopkins village. They went to a fancy resort they had seen and shared a few Pina Coladas and grilled lobsters together to celebrate. It was a memorable night.

Chapter 17 - Finding the Maya

The honeymoon in Belize was everything Dan and Susan had hoped for, and more. Unfortunately time was running out. Soon they would be heading back to the USA and the work-a-day world. Dan and Susan had to decide whether to spend their last two days at the beach or visit the missionaries near Orange Walk. After several discussions they felt called to visit the missionaries. They knew they would have future opportunities to lie on a beach somewhere in the world, but when would they ever be invited to visit a Mayan village and see what American missionaries are doing? Off they went to San Carlos Village near Orange Walk in northern Belize. From Hopkins, this was a three hour ride so they arrived, just before noon.

They had no idea how to find Harry in this small village so they stopped the first person they saw along the road. He was a tiny old man carrying a long machete. "Excuse me," Dan said, "Do you know where the American missionaries are staying in this village?"

The man looked at them for a long time. "No speak English," he responded.

"Americano missionarioes?" Dan loudly asked again, trying to sound Spanish.

The man looked at them and pointed at the crossroad ahead of them. He softly muttered, "Gringos." Then he walked away. So Dan and Susan followed the directions and in two blocks they were at a concrete block house with three white vans parked in front. Dan recognized the vans from the rental agency at the airport. He parked next to the vans. Dan and Susan went up to the front of the house.

Harry came out the door smiling with his arms outstretched. He embraced Dan and Susan. "Well, praise God," Harry shouted. "This is a surprise. We hoped you might visit us. Are you hungry? You are just in time for lunch."

"We really want to see what you are doing in Belize," Susan replied. "We would love to have lunch with you, but we don't want to impose."

"Don't be silly," Harry responded. "Veronica makes enough to feed an army. We're having the specialty of Belize today, rice and beans. Do you like rice and beans? And be sure to try the pineapple. It will knock your socks off. They grow them here you know. Come on in. Let's find you some grub and a place to sit.

They went to the serving area where Dan and Susan were given plates loaded with rice and beans. The chief cook, Veronica, offered them some homemade salsa. The other Belizean serving woman said something about 'caliente' to warn them about the salsa as Dan heaped it on his rice. Dan paid no attention to the warning. Susan was more careful with the salsa. The room was filled with the din of many conversations going on at once. Harry found them a couple of plastic chairs in the crowded room and sat at the table. As they began to eat, they glanced around the room There must have been more than two dozen people eating in this small room at three tables. Everyone was sweaty and dirty. They were all talking at once and eating at the same time.

Harry banged on the table. "Everyone, listen up!" Harry announced. "This is Dan and Susan. They have come on an inspection tour, so be on your best behavior." Some mumbled their mock agreement. "Really, they just are visiting and want to see what we are doing. I'm going to show them around and hopefully they will stay for the fiesta tonight. Introduce yourselves." Everyone took turns greeting them.

People passed around bowls of sliced pineapple and papaya. The fruit was exceptionally sweet and delicious. Susan noticed Dan's forehead was covered in sweat beads. "Are you okay?" Susan asked. Dan just nodded. Someone at their table passed Susan two glasses and a pitcher of orange colored drink. Susan poured the glasses full and handed one to Dan. He grabbed it and poured the whole glassful down his throat. The people at their table started giggling. Susan filled his glass three times as he kept emptying the glass.

In a teasing tone a woman across from Dan asked him, "How do like Veronica's special salsa?"

Dan tried to smile, but it was pitiful. When he tried to speak his tongue was not working. With much effort he finally got out the word he was trying to speak, "Hot!"

Everyone burst out laughing. They had noticed the heap of salsa on his rice and were waiting for him to take a few bites. This was a normal rite of initiation for new comers.

Dan pushed the salsa to the end of his plate and ate the rice that had not contacted it. When he looked up he saw Susan shaking her head, and giving him her look. The look was a 'I-told-you-so' kind of look. Fortunately, Dan found the pineapple helped put out the fire in his throat and tongue.

After lunch everybody started drifting away to their work places.

"Come on and see what we're doing," Harry invited. He led Dan and Susan through some yards to a house that was being painted. It was sixteen feet by twenty feet, made of concrete block, and covered with stucco. The pitched roof was of aluminum laminate. "This is a house we're just completing for Pedro and Sophia Eck. They have six children. That is thier old house over there." He pointed to a small building made of upright sticks with a thatch roof of palm leaves. "Pedro has been waiting four years for this house," Harry added. "He has been working on our other houses to qualify for his house. We call it 'sweat equity.' Pedro also bought the five hundred blocks as his contribution to getting a home. Would you like to meet Pedro?"

"Absolutely!" Dan responded. "What kind of work does Pedro do?"

"He cuts sugar cane," Harry answered. "Most of the men in this village cut cane. The average family income is about one thousand US dollars a year. Not really enough to support a family, but they manage to survive. Hey, Pedro. I want you to meet my friends from Kentucky. This is Susan and Dan."

"Thank you for seeing my house," Pedro said. "You come inside and see how nice." They all went inside where a few people were finishing the painting of the interior. The house was divided into three rooms with a wooden partition. Pedro introduced Susan and Dan to two children covered in paint who were working furiously pushing rollers of white latex on the walls. "Juan is my oldest boy. He have fourteen years. He graduated from St Vincent School this year number two in his class. Carla have nine years and she in St. Vincent School. My little children in school. They all happy to have this house."

"We are so please to meet you," Susan said as she shook the hands of the children. They smiled and returned to their work. "Pedro, where is your wife?"

"Sophia, you meet?" Pedro asked.

"No, we have not meet, Sophia," Susan answered. "I mean met Sophia. But we would like to meet her."

"Oh!" Pedro replied. "She in house making lunch. You have lunch in house? She help Veronica. You meet Sophia now."

"We will introduce ourselves to her later," Dan interjected. He could see there was some miscommunication going on. He asked Pedro if they could go into his old house. Pedro nodded in agreement and led them into his old house. Dan and Susan were surprised by the lack of furniture. Hammocks were hanging against the walls. Plastic sacks containing clothing were hanging from the rafters. There was a small wooden table and two plastic chairs. The table was covered with school books. In a corner was a tiny television on concrete blocks linked to a car battery. An old curtain divided part of the tiny house into a separate space. The floor was dirt.

"I make," Pedro said with pride.

"You made this house?" Susan asked.

"I make it," Pedro repeated.

"When you make?" Dan asked.

"Humm." Pedro thought for a moment and said, "Maybe before Juan come. I get palmetto in bush and build strong house. Sophia no like living in my father's house too much. Too many my brother's children. He make six children. Sophia want own house. So I make house for her. You know Ramiro, my brother?"

"Uh, sorry we have not met your brother," Susan answered. "Maybe we will meet him later." Dan and Susan thanked Pedro for showing them his house. They walked back to the new house. They noticed Pedro had some missing fingers, but did not feel comfortable asking him about why he was missing fingers.

When Pedro left them they asked Harry, "How did Pedro lose his fingers?

"Most of the men who cut cane have missing fingers," Harry replied. "They work from sunrise to sundown six days a week when the work is available and sometimes they hit their fingers with the machetes. They all have many scars on their legs from machete cuts. When they do that they just keep working. Most of these people never go to the hospital or see a doctor because they can't afford it. That's why we bring these doctors to do village clinics. We provide some free medical care. It's not enough; but, for many people, it's more than they would ever have otherwise."

"How old is Pedro?" Susan asked. "He looks to be sixty-five to seventy at least."

"Pedro is forty-one," Harry answered.

Dan and Susan were shocked. "I never would have guessed it," Susan said

"Hard work and poor diet," Harry stated, "ages these people. He has worked very hard as a cane cutter since he was a child. His diet has been almost exclusively rice and beans. He has never seen a doctor in his life. The average life expectancy is fifty years here, so he is trying to raise his children before his life ends. All of his children attend school. His dream is that his children will have the opportunity to attend high school so they can have a better life than his."

"Will his children go to high school?" Susan asked. "I mean, they seem bright. Why wouldn't they go to high school?"

"High school is not free in Belize," Harry answered. "It costs about five hundred dollars a year to send a child to high school when you add the tuition, book fees, bus fare, and uniforms all together. Pedro only makes a little over a thousand dollars a year cutting cane. That's what the family lives on. There isn't enough to send one child to high school. That is why we provide some scholarships for students to go to high school. Of course, we only do what we can. Our resources are limited and this is just one small village and there are hundreds of villages just like it!"

The grim reality of Pedro's life and the lack of opportunity for his children laid heavy on the hearts of Susan and Dan. They were having trouble dealing with the reality before them. Dan and Susan stopped asking questions for awhile. The reality of Pedro's life and his family was a challenge for Dan and Susan to process. They walked around the village and visited a few other families. Some had small nice homes while others had primitive houses like Pedro's old house. They found all the people they met to be friendly and uncomplaining. The children were all remarkably clean and appeared happy. It was evident from the numerous holy pictures on the walls of the homes that people had a relationship with God. After walking around the village, Dan and Susan were disturbed.

"It's just not fair," Susan said to Dan. "How can a man work so hard and have so little? Why can't his children have a chance to go to school? Why do we have so much and they have so little? It's just not right!?"

"There are millions of families like Pedro's family all over the world," Dan said. "I've seen poverty worst than this in other parts of the world. It's overwhelming. The problem is too big. It just makes you grateful for how good we have it. There's nothing we can do about it."

Susan stopped and looked directly into Dan's eyes. "I hope you don't really mean that," Susan shot back at Dan. "Did you see the house they are building for Pedro? Did you see his children? Do you think Harry and this group of Americans are making a difference? How can you say there is nothing we can do? I don't believe you mean that!"

"Susan, slow down," Dan said defensively. "I just mean, I can't change the world. There are billions of poor people. The problem of global economic inequity is beyond my capacity to change it. I wish I could tithe at church, but I can't even do that with my business on the ropes. Susan, I have a responsibility to take care of you and Troy and Dianna now. What more can you expect from me? I wish I could do more, but I'm tapped out."

"Dan," Susan looking into his eyes said, "I know you are doing the best you can, and I do believe in you. But I need you to trust me in this. I want to tell Pedro we will help him with the money to send his children to high school. I know that God will help us find a way to do this. After all, it's just a few hundred dollars a year. It is something I have to do. I cannot walk away from this village and do nothing. God has laid this burden on my heart and I cannot turn my back on Pedro and his family."

"I hear you," Dan said as he dropped his eyes to the ground. They were quiet for awhile. Dan though about things before he said, "We should talk to Harry, and ask him how we can go about making the arrangements. You're right on this. I love your compassion. I was trying to rationalize my way out of here without doing anything. Thank God you listened to the Holy Spirit and not to me!"

That afternoon they talked to Harry about how the scholarship funding worked and made a pledge to help with the funding for Pedro's children to go to high school. Harry was insistent they stay for the fiesta and worship that evening. Dan and Susan declined the offer because they had a three hour drive back to

Hopkins and didn't want to stay overnight in San Carlos. They were emotionally exhausted. They went by the house that was being painted and said goodbye to Pedro, Juan, and Carla. They mentioned the scholarship money to Pedro. He looked at them in disbelief, and then his expression changed to joy as they reassured him it was true. Pedro was very happy. He ran off to tell his family.

They found a cute little restaurant to have a small supper in Orange Walk after leaving San Carlos. Susan asked Dan if he wanted more salsa on his food. Dan smiled weakly.

It was late when they arrived back in Hopkins, and they went right to bed. They were emotionally exhausted. The next day they relaxed and enjoy their last day of honeymoon on the beach. That night they were in complete agreement about everything and passionately concluded their honeymoon.

Chapter 18 - Re-entry

Upon returning to the United States were surprised by their emotional responses. The wealth of this country compared to Belize was so evident in everything they experienced from landing at Houston airport to driving on the interstate from the airport in Cincinnati to home. As they pulled into the garage at their house Dan realized his garage was bigger than the homes they saw in the villages. As Dan looked at all the miscellaneous tools and equipment he had in his garage compared to the scarcity of such things in the villages in Belize he felt uneasy with his all possessions he took for granted. Susan thought about all the shoes and dresses she had owned that were lost in the fire. She had more clothes than all the women in the village combined. When she went into her kitchen and thought about all of the appliances that she found indispensable, and compared that dependence on machines to the women in Belize who owned no appliances. Dan and Susan had a big cultural adjustment to make and it was going to take time for them to transition back to the wealth of the United States..

Susan and Dan were enthusiastically greeted by their children and Susan's sister who had waiting up for their arrival past midnight. Mindy jumped all over Dan and almost wagged herself apart.

Susan gave Troy a carved wooden dolphin she had bought in Belize. She gave Dianna a Mayan embroidered dress that had bright flowers on a plain white background. Dianna said she would wear it to school the next day. Susan's sister was given a beautiful amber bracelet they had purchased in San Ignacio. The next evening, Dan loaded his photos of their honeymoon into his notebook computer and showed them on the flat screen television and showed some of pictures they had taken. When they got to the dozens of photos of furniture he had taken at Peters' factory the children soon got bored. He had to skip through them and get to the Mayan ruins. They enjoyed recounting the wonder of discovering that ancient culture. As they looked at the photos of Pedro and his village Dan and Susan both realized it was impossible to express what that visit had meant to them. They both agreed that Troy and Dianna needed to visit Belize in the future to experience it for themselves. It had become after ten o'clock and Susan and the kids had school the next day so they went to bed. Dan and Susan were so grateful to be home and sleeping in the comfort of their own bed.

The next morning Dan started to organize his furniture photos for a presentation he would send electronically to the Arens furniture company in California. He tried his best to match the photos with descriptions of the type of wood and to quote a price that include cost, transportation, and profit. He had taken copious notes in Belize so it was possible to match the type of wood and cost with the photographs. Considering what the retail mark-up would be in California, he had to keep the wholesale price reasonable he was charging. After working all day, he sent the information to the prospective buyer.

What was critical to his importing the furniture was the availability of containers in Shipyard. This meant Mr. Peters could pack an order at his factory, have the container transported to Belize City, it would be loaded on a ship, transported to Fort Lauderdale, Florida, received by a shipping company, put on a railroad car, and taken anyplace in the United States. In theory an order could be delivered in a matter of weeks. The use of containers has revolutionized the import business. Transport of containers was all computerized which perfect tracking of merchandise. Of course nothing ever worked that easily in reality.

In the weeks that followed, Dan and Susan began talking about taking a youth group on a mission trip to Belize in a year or two. They were so full of enthusiasm for the idea, they talked about it to everyone they met at Hartwell Church. They found the reactions to their suggestion at church about the mission trip to be widely mixed. Some people were enthusiastically supportive of the idea, some were indifferent, and surprisingly some people were fairly opposed to the idea. Dan and Susan tried to not be discouraged by the less supportive reactions and continued promoting the mission trip at Hartwell Church. There was a consensus of opinion they would need at least a year and a half for fundraising so they had ample time to plan. Pastor Andy became one of their biggest supporters, which was a huge factor in the success of the venture. The pastor assured them many times that the funding would come when they needed it. In time a core of people committed to the mission experience developed at the church.

While Dan and Susan talked incessantly about organizing a youth mission trip to Belize they missed what their children were hiding from the. Troy and Dianna were reluctant to tell their mother about the times their father had met with them while they had been away on their honeymoon. At every visit he had tried to persuade them to live with him. Dianna being a teenager was less persuaded by her father's appeals than Troy. Troy was younger and still eager to please his father. They had evaded his demands and were sworn to secrecy by their father to not tell their mother or step father. Susan had suspected that something was troubling them and asked them if they wanted to tell her anything. They denied there was a problem. Troy and Dianna had several conversations about the dilemma they faced. After a few weeks they decided to tell Susan.

"Mom," Dianna began, "we don't want to make you mad. We have to tell you something, but we promised Dad we would keep it a secret. We don't know what to do. So Troy and I have decided to tell you, even though we promised not to tell. Dad wants us to leave you and live with him. He has said things about you and Dan that are really bad." Dianna began to cry. Troy looked at his feet in embarrassment.

"Sweetheart, it's alright," Susan said putting her hand on Dianna's hand. "Just tell me what you need to say. The truth is the most important thing. I want to know what is going on." Dianna was silent because she didn't know what to say or how to say it.

"He hates you and Dan," Troy blurted out. "He really can't stand Dan. He thinks you are fake Christians. He thinks we're all going to hell because we're phonies. He keeps talking about apostasy and hypocrisy, and I don't even know what that means. What is it?"

"He thinks we believe in the wrong things," Susan answered. "He has no respect for Hartwell Church or the pastor. That is his opinion. Honestly , the thing that makes him mad is not our religious differences. He wants to control us and he uses religion as his justification. This is not really about whose faith is right or true. This is about his emotional need to be the boss."

"But Mom," Dianna emphatically said, "How do you know what he thinks? He says he only wants what is best for us. He prays for our salvation all the time. You know he loves the Lord. He says he only wants us to know Jesus and to be saved."

"I'm sure that's what he believes," Dianna answered calmly. "Do you believe I love Jesus? Don't you think Dan loves Jesus? Do the people at Hartwell Church love Jesus? Who is he to deny our faith or sincerity?"

"I believe you, but....." Dianna stopped there.

"Dan and I have never tried to turn you and Troy against your father," Susan said trying to help her children understand the situation, "but you have to trust me. Your father has problems that we can't fix. He is using religion to manipulate you. It is important that you understand that. You know I am not the person he says I am. He is desperate to have you both and will say anything and do anything to get you away from me and Dan."

"Dianna and me don't want to leave you," Troy said. "We do like Dan and we want to stay here. It's hard listening to dad. He's so sure about everything. He tells us stuff from the Bible to prove he's right! He's kind of scary sometimes."

"Promise me," Susan responded, "you will not keep secrets from me. Your father has no right to make you promise to have secrets from me. If he asks you to do that, you need to tell him you will not keep things from me. I understand that will make him angry. He won't like it. But, he is not going to drive a wedge between us. We are not going to play his game. I will always be honest with you and I expect you both to be honest with me. Is that fair?"

Dianna and Troy nodded their agreement.

That night after Dianna and Troy went to bed, Susan told him about the conversation she had with Troy and Dianna in as much detail as she could recall. She then added, "I don't know if I handled it right or not, but I did the best I could."

"I think you handled it brilliantly," Dan replied. "You told them the truth, and they will have to sort it out for themselves. You know in my study of Christian history this is the same old story. People use the faith to control other people for their own agendas. It sickens me when people use the Bible to beat up people. It's no wonder people see the church as dysfunctional. When I read Jesus praying, 'May they all be one as we are one,' I just don't know what he thinks of us. Is it blasphemy to use God that way? Is this really the sin against the Holy Spirit?"

"That's beyond me," Susan answered. "I know it's not right to use faith to mess with children the way Jay's doing it."

"In time Troy and Dianna will figure this out for themselves," Dan said. "We're not always going to be there to protect them, but they have a solid foundation to figure things out for themselves. It's unfair they're subjected to this problem. All we can do is love them, pray for them, and trust in them. Jay can't harm us." When Dan said that, his mind immediately flashed to the image of the burning house. He was convinced Jay had set the fire even though there was no evidence to convict him of the crime. Dan refused to speculate on what harm Jay was capable of. He clearly was not going to alarm Susan with any thoughts he might have about Jay's possible schemes.

Over the next couple of days Dan pondered about ways he could protect his family. He could only come up with one practical plan. He would do everything to improve communications with Troy and Dianna in the hope he would be able to intervene, if necessary, when appropriate.

The rain was coming down hard when Dianna left school that afternoon. She had her book bag over her head to keep the rain off. As she rushed to the parking lot to find her ride home, she heard her name shouted from a car. When she looked in the direction of the shout she saw her father's white sedan. She ran over to his car and he yelled, "Jump in!" After she got in Jay began, "Hey beautiful, how yah doing? Just wanted to talk to you for a minute."

"What's up dad?" Dianna asked.

"I was praying about you and Troy this morning," Jay said, "and the Lord laid some concerns on my heart. Are you okay? How's life been treating you?"

"I'm good," Dianna answered. "How you doing?"

"Great! Praise God! I'm great," Jay responded, "Have you thought about what I asked you to consider last week? I am not going to give you any more time to decide. You know the Lord is coming back soon and we all have to decide where we stand."

"Dad, you need to know something," Dianna answered. "Troy and I have to talked to mom about......"

"I told you not to tell her!" Jay snapped. "What did you tell that woman?"

"We talked about everything you said," Dianna bravely answered. "Mom loves Jesus and she is doing the best she can to follow him. Troy and I are staying with Mom. Dad I love you too, but I am not leaving Mom. And Troy feels the same as me."

Jay glared at her. He was not prepared for this rejection. He was trembling trying to control the rage that was swelling up inside him. "You little whore," he sneered at her. "So she has turned you against me. Now it's out in the open. She has no idea who she has let loose. Let this be upon her in judgment. Whore of Babylon reigns for a season and then the fall."

"Dad, stop it!" Dianna shouted. "You're acting really weird. I'm going to miss my ride." Dianna started to open the car door. "Gotta go now!"

"You know not what you do!" Jay stated flatly. "This is all your doing now. You force this upon me. So be it!"

As Dianna stepped out of the car Jay pulled away before she had a chance to close the door. The car door swung wide open as he roared out of the parking lot. Dianna ran across the parking lot to her friends waiting car and got in sobbing.

When Susan got home Dianna was waiting to tell her what had happened with Jay. Susan couldn't make sense of Jay's remarks. Dianna got frustrated and confused trying to recount exactly the things he said. Susan was very distressed at how visibly upset Dianna became remembering the incident. Susan tried to comfort her, but was at a loss to rationally explain the meaning of Jay's words. After Dianna was calmed down and went to her room Susan sat for a long while and pondered what Jay had said. She picked up the phone and called her attorney and explained the situation. He immediately suggested they get a restraining order to keep Jay away from troy and Dianna. Susan was reluctant at first, but the attorney sensed a danger to the family in the veiled threats and was persistent. Susan finally agreed and the attorney handled the details of getting a restraining order.

While all of this was going on, Dan had been out at his bank and making arrangements with a shipping company concerning furniture arriving in Florida from Belize. That afternoon he had a call from the retailer in California asking for a selection of items from Mr. Peters' factory. They wanted enough pieces to fill a small container shipped as soon as possible. Dan had called Mr. Peters' phone and e-mailed him the order. Mr. Peters had given him his bank account number so Dan could wire the money directly to his account. Dan had gone to his bank and had the money transferred to Mr. Peters' account. Then he visited the shipping company in person to make certain they were clear on the pick-up, transportation, and delivery of the container when it arrived in Florida. Dan was not worried about fronting the payment because he knew the retailer was good for the order. He was confident they would place a substantial order after they received the sample pieces. His years of experience told him he was on to something big. He was not going to waste any time following up on this opportunity.

When Dan got home, Susan told him what had happened to Dianna that afternoon with Jay Dan was deeply disturbed by what he heard. Susan then told him about contacting the attorney and the restraining order. Dan was greatly relieved when he heard that outcome. "I only wish we had done that sooner," he said. "I had no idea he was that far gone! Now he won't be able to get near them and make any more threats. This will chill him out. Do you think Dianna is going to be okay?"

"Dianna is really upset," Susan answered. "But she's stronger than you think. She'll handle it. The thing is, I don't know how I'm going to deal with it!" She collapsed into Dan's arms and he held her tight for a long time.

Chapter 19 - The Crash

Over the many months Dan and Susan had been working at the soup kitchen, the composition of the meals had changed dramatically. More and more churches had become involved in both procuring donations and providing workers to prepare the meals. It was typical for them to offer a choice of vegetables and entrees to the several hundred people who came for the Saturday meal. Dan and Susan found several people who wanted to be completely responsible for the meal on specific Saturdays so they had some days off. Rev Bob no longer was responsible for procuring or preparing the food so he spent his time on other parts of his urban ministry. As the word spread about the soup kitchen they actually had a surplus of churches wanting to serve and sufficient funds to invest in upgrading the kitchen at the church. What had been a burden on the handful of people who had run the feeding program became a blessing for many people as an opportunity to serve the poor.

Dan and Susan had not seen or heard from Jay for two months since they had the restraining order put on him. Dianna and Troy began to relax from the anxiety of his surprise visits. They loved their father but hated the pressure he put on them to leave their mother. Dan and Susan assumed he had moved on from his obsession to regain his children. They were unaware he had sold his car and was driving a small pickup truck. None of them noticed him watching their movements from safe distances.

The furniture imported from Belize was the business success Dan had hoped it would be. The only problem was the ability of Mr. Peters and his craftsmen to keep up with the orders. They had several close relations working on different types of furniture. They were becoming more specialized, with one family making chairs, another tables, and another bureaus. The Mennonites are very ingenious and constantly inventing new ways to be more efficient. They began to employ more Belizeans to supplement their workforce. It was all good for everyone involved.

Susan had to attend a meeting in Columbus State Educators Association as the union representative for her school. She had tried to find another teacher who was going to the same meeting but was unable to connect with anyone. The two hour drive on the interstate was tedious because the road is so straight and flat running through miles of cornfields occasionally broken by soybean fields. The meeting went until four-thirty in the afternoon which put her in the middle of the Columbus rush hour. It took her almost an hour to get out of the Columbus gridlock and on her way to Kentucky. She stopped halfway home at Washington Courthouse and had some dinner and coffee to keep her alert for the remaining hour drive home. She never noticed the rental truck following her. The sun had just gone down and the traffic was sparse. Susan was listening to National Public Radio, the program's guest was talking about the struggles of women in Afghanistan. The large box truck pulled alongside her in the passing lane and suddenly lurched into her lane. She felt the front of her car jolted to the right from the impact and she automatically pulled the wheel to the right to avoid the looming truck. She was going seventy miles per hour when she turned a hard right. Her car began to roll down the highway until she ended in the cornfield several hundred feet from where she had been hit. The driver of the rental van continued down the highway ignoring the incident. Susan was strapped in her seat and experienced the car rolling over as if time had slowed to a crawl. She could only think how surreal it was going from right side up to upside down over and over. It felt like it would never end. She could feel the seat belt cutting into her ribs. It wasn't until the front of the car impacted the soft ground of the cornfield did the airbag go off slamming her in the face. "Jesus," she cried out, "help me." That's when she lost consciousness.

A truck driver who was a quarter mile behind her was the first person on the scene. He stopped his truck on the side of the road and put some flares down to warn other drivers. He rushed over to Susan's car which was upside down and tried to open the driver's side door. He was worried that the car might catch fire and Susan was hanging upside down inside. The door was locked shut. He went to the passenger side and tried to open that door. It was also locked.

Another motorist had stopped and rushed to the scene. "We've got to get her out of there!" he shouted to the onlookers who had just arrived.

"The dam doors are stuck," the truck driver yelled back to the people approaching the accident. "I think she's out. But this car may go any minute!"

"I'm gonna bust the window," said the other man. "Let's get her out of there!" He shattered the window with a piece of metal he found on the side of the road. The truck driver unlocked the door from the inside. He yanked the door and tried to free Susan hanging in upside down trapped in her seatbelt. The truck driver couldn't get the releasing mechanism of the seat belt to operate. He took out his pocket knife and cut her shoulder strap and waist strap while the other man supported her. As gently as possible they lifted her out of the car and laid her on the ground. More people were arriving on the scene. Some were discussing how had called 911 and reported the accident. Others were telling the men not to move Susan.

"I'm a nurse," a woman said entering the group standing around Susan as she lay on the ground. Some of the people backed off a little ways. Susan's face was covered in blood. The nurse checked Susan's vital signs and announced she was breathing and had a pulse. "Does anyone have a blanket we could put on her?" the nurse asked the crowd. Quickly a woman raced to her car and got a blanket to cover Susan to keep her warm. They decided there was not much they could do until the ambulance arrived. Someone brought a blanket and covered Susan's legs. Soon an emergency medical team arrived and followed by an ambulance. They checked her vital signs, and then they carefully placed Susan on a back board and carried her into the ambulance. They took her to the nearest hospital which was Walker Baptist Hospital just north of Cincinnati. She was rushed to emergency and examined by several doctors. They determined she had ruptured her spleen and had several broken ribs. Her face was lacerated, but nothing was broken. The concussion was not too severe. They decided to operate on her immediately to remove her spleen and keep her from becoming septic.

The police had arrived at the scene of the accident at the same time as the ambulance. Fortunately the people who reported the accident to 911 had told them there was a woman badly injured and trapped in her car. The police had found Susan's driver's license and had called Dan at home. He raced to the hospital. The whole way there he kept repeating aloud, "O Lord, don't let anything happen to my precious Susan. Help her Jesus!" Somehow he reached the hospital, going eighty miles an hour, without getting stopped. When he arrived Susan was already in surgery. One of the emergency room doctors, who had examined her, told him she was going to be fine and they were going to remove her spleen and look for any other internal injuries. The doctor seemed confident there was nothing to worry about. He said the cuts to her face were superficial. He assured Dan he could relax and wait for the surgeons to finish the operation for a complete condition report. Dan paced the surgical waiting area like a caged animal. After an hour wait the surgeon came out and asked Dan to join him in a consulting room. The small windowless room closed in on Dan. "Susan is doing well," the surgeon said. "She has been through a massive trauma which ruptured her spleen. She lost a lot of blood internally. We removed the spleen and washed her abdominal cavity with saline solution. There was some bruising to her kidneys but they should function normally and heal on their own. Right now she needs rest. We are giving her antibiotics to prevent infection intravenously. Her condition is stable and the prognosis is very good. We expect a full recovery. Do you have any questions?"

"When can I see her?" Dan asked. "I can't believe this happened. Are you sure she is going to be fine?"

"She is doing well, considering what she has been through," the surgeon replied. "We are always concerned about infection with an internal injury like this. Hopefully we got her cleaned up and nothing will develop. She's going to be in recovery for a while and then we will take her to surgical intensive care. You'll be able to see her there."

Dan thanked the surgeon and sat down in the waiting area. After some time he remembered he had rushed out of the house without telling Troy or Dianna what was going on. He didn't want to tell them over the phone, but he wasn't going to leave the hospital so he decided to call them. "Dianna," he said, "I have something important to tell you. Your mother was in a car accident and she is in the hospital in Cincinnati. She has just had surgery and the doctor says she is doing fine." Dianna kept interrupting him with questions. She was understandably upset. Dan tried to answer her questions and calm her with some small success. Eventually he was exhausted with Dianna's questions and he realized he was going to address the same issues with Troy. He asked to speak to Troy and talked to him for another forty-five minutes. Sometime later the nurse came out and found him. She said he could see her for a couple of minutes in the SICU. He followed her down the hall and through the double doors.

Much of Susan's face was bandaged. Her eyes were closed. She was covered up to her neck by a sheet except for her arms which lay neatly on either side with the palms up. There were IV's in each arm, a blood oxygen monitor on a finger, and multiple colored wrist bands. Nurses were busy in the room adjusting a vast array of equipment. Dan leaned over and kissed Susan on the forehead. "Susan, my love," he said softly. "Susan, I love you." Susan's eyes fluttered. "I'm here sweetheart," Dan whispered. "You are doing good. You're going to be all right." Susan opened her eyes and looked at Dan. She gave a slight hint of a smile and her eyes closed. "I love you," Dan repeated. The nurse came over to Dan.

"Can you give us some time with her?" the nurse asked. "We have more to do."

Dan looked at the nurse. He realized he was an obstruction to their work and, reluctantly, he left the room. He looked around the room at the numerous machines with tubes and wires.

Electronic displays were flashing numbers and some were beeping. The nurses were rushing around making adjustments. Hanging next to the bed was a cluster of plastic bags filled with liquids that fed into Susan's arm. He realized he was an obstruction to their work, and he left the room.

Alone in the waiting area Dan sat in a chair and prayed. "God, how could you do this to her. She did nothing to deserve this. Where were you when she needed you? Haven't we done enough for you? She is the most loving person and you let her go through this? How can you allow it to happen? Heal her now! I can't believe you let this happen to her of all people."

The more Dan prayed the angrier he became. He had no idea how the accident happened. He had no one to blame but God. God was getting all his pain and rage. That night Dan was allowed to visit Susan for several more brief visits. She slept soundly because of the narcotics being pumped into her to numb the trauma of the accident and surgery. Her condition was stable.

Morning came. Dan looked at his watch and realized he had only slept a couple of hours during the night. He went to the hospital cafeteria and ate a small breakfast and drank several cups of coffee. When he returned to the SICU waiting area he was surprised to find Pastor Andy. Without words Pastor Andy embraced him. Dan eventually pulled away. "This should never have happened to Susan," Dan said.

"How is she?" Pastor Andy said.

"The doctor told me she is doing well," Dan responded, "considering the injuries," Dan responded. They then discussed in details the injuries as best Dan could remember. Pastor Andy asked if he could visit her, and Dan suggested they call the nurse and ask permission. They were allowed back into the SICU area. Pastor Andy gently held Susan's hand and prayed quietly for her and Dan. When they were about to leave Dan kissed Susan on the lips and she opened her eyes.

"Hi, darling," she said looking searchingly into Dan's eyes. "How are you?"

"I'm good," Dan answered as tears fell from his eyes. "How are you feeling?"

"Oh, very sleepy," Susan said. "How are Troy and Dianna? Are they okay?" Then she coughed and her face grimaced with pain. "Maybe I should have come home sooner."

"Everyone is fine," Dan said, "We're all worried about you. We just want you to get better. Does it hurt?"

"The left side of my chest feels like there is a truck parked on it," Susan whispered. Then she noticed Pastor Andy standing behind Dan. "Hey where did you come from?"

"Just dropped by to see how you're doing," he replied.

"Thanks for being here," Susan said. "Will you take care of Dan?"

"Of course," he answered. "But we need you to get well."

Susan's eyes began to close and she smiled as she drifted back asleep.

Dan and Pastor Andy left the SICU and went back to the waiting area. They talked about the accident. Dan was openly questioning God and the unfairness of this horrible accident. Pastor Andy realized he could not persuade Dan of God's ultimate goodness in the state of mind Dan was in. He told Dan to give his feelings to God and God would understand. He also told Andy he needed to get some rest. It would not be good for Susan for him to be exhausted. Pastor Andy suggested he go home and talk to the children and get some sleep. Dan didn't respond to the suggestion.

Dan stayed at the hospital all that day and made periodic visits to Susan. She was more frequently awake during these visits. The powerful medications given her during surgery were wearing off. She was experiencing increasing pain and tried hard not to show it to Dan. He was aware she was suffering. That evening he went home barely able to drive. He talked to the children when he got home and went to bed.

Chapter 20 - Fall From Grace

Two days after the surgery, Susan's condition turned rapidly worse. She began to develop a high fever and her abdomen became distended. It was immediately apparent to the doctors she had developed an infection in her abdomen which was a result of the ruptured spleen. She had three broken ribs on the left side. Susan was becoming weak and was having trouble speaking.

Dan was constantly with her except when he went home at night to be with Troy and Dianna. He brought the children for visits in the evening with their mother, but they were brief because she was in SICU. The doctor informed him that her condition was considered critical. Dan fully understood her life was in eminent danger. There were visits by family and church members to the hospital, but they were discouraged because of the strict limitations of the SICU. Mostly the visitors spent their time with Dan in the waiting room. Although many tried to help Dan process this senseless catastrophe, Dan was stuck in anger. He did not confide his feelings with his visitors because he was ashamed to admit how he felt. He was sullen and unresponsive when people talked about their faith and prayed with him.

The police report on the accident was factual and vague because there were no witnesses to the accident other than Susan and the driver of the truck. Susan remembered nothing about the accident and was not interested in talking about it. The truck driver was never heard from. The drivers of the cars that came upon the scene of the accident were too far away to see what had happened. The police only had the skid marks of Susan's vehicle to measure and photograph. This left Dan assuming that this was a senseless random accident. He turned all of his frustration and fears upon God. It appeared to be completely without purpose or explanation. He decided if the universe was so random and cruel, then God was either indifferent or possibly non-existent. He was constantly being reminded by visitors and phone calls that people were praying for Susan. He thanked people for their prayers, but secretly thought praying was a futile gesture. He felt totally abandoned by God.

On the fourth day after the accident he was alone with Susan. He thought she was sleeping. "God is with me!" She suddenly said to Dan with her eyes opening wide. "He is going to heal me and I feel His love in me. The Lord is with me!"

Dan didn't know what to say. He immediately assumed she was hallucinating. "The doctors are doing everything they can," he said, "to get you better."

"I know that," Susan replied. "The doctors and nurses are wonderful. They are the hands of Jesus who called them to be his healers. But they cannot do what God is doing. God is working a healing and I am going to get well." She stopped and grabbed Dan's hand. "And I am praying our Jesus will work a miracle in you, my love."

Dan was frightened by what Susan said. *How could she know* he thought to *himself what is happening with me. How could she possibly know?* But Dan knew she somehow was aware of the battle raging within him. He couldn't lie to her, and he was not going to admit the truth. He struggled to think of something to say. "I'm doing fine," Dan finally said. "It's you I am concerned about."

"Darling, I know you are worried about me," Susan answered. "You can give that to the Lord. This is when we need Him. This is not the time to turn your back on God. Dan, give it all to Him. He will carry your burden. I want you to unload what you're carrying on Him."

Dan changed the subject to the children's school work. Susan understood she had challenged him enough for now. After a while he left her so she could rest. While he was waiting, Susan's nurse came out of the SICU. "Dr. Gibran is making his rounds," she said, "and this might be a good opportunity to speak with him." Dan went back into the SICU and found Doctor Gibran who was the specialist in charge of Susan. He asked about her condition.

"Last night the kidney and liver numbers were very bad," Dr. Gibran said. "We were hoping for better numbers today and we have gotten just now the results of the blood tests from this morning."

"What are her numbers?" Dan interrupted.

"That is what I am trying to tell you!" Dr. Gibran continued. "There has been some improvement in the kidney and liver numbers. We are cautiously optimist she has turned the corner. You know, we have done everything we can do; but, it is out of our hands at this stage. She has a strong faith which makes a big difference. I have to give God the credit because it's a miracle she survived the night. I've been praying for her and I'm sure our prayers are being answered. God is good."

"Thank you Doctor," Dan said. He had nothing else to say to the doctor. He walked quickly to Susan's room. He found Susan fast asleep and sat in the chair next to the bed. He went over in his mind the emotions he had felt the past few days and was so ashamed at what he had been through in his mind. He began to talk to God. "Lord Jesus, You should despise me. I'm a fool and I have betrayed you in my anger against you. I deserve whatever you want to do with me. Can you forgive me? Why would you ever forgive me because I am so undeserving? Please, heal my precious wife for her sake. I am not asking to do it for me. I deserve your contempt, but she has never stopped loving you. Even in the valley of death, you are with her. Have mercy on me Jesus. I'm a sinner." Dan was weeping. He quietly recited the Lord's Prayer with his head in his hands. When he finished and looked up, Susan was smiling at him.

"Did I wake you?" Dan said wiping the tears from his face.

"God is so good, my love!" Susan answered. "I knew you could not stay mad at God for long. He told me about you and I have asked him to heal you. And He is faithful."

"I wish I had your faith, dearest," Dan replied.

"There is nothing wrong with your faith," Susan said. "You were tested and you have come out of it with a stronger faith. Do you mind if I sleep a little? I'm so tired."

Dan watched Susan fall asleep. He stayed awhile and watched over her. He kept thanking God for healing her. Although she was still fighting the infection, he was certain she was going to recover. After an hour he left the hospital and called Pastor Andy on his cell phone. "Hey, this is Dan," he said. "I know you are probably busy, but is there any way I could stop by and see you this afternoon. I need to talk with you."

Pastor Andy said he would be glad to see him and to come over. Pastor Andy had an appointment with the church treasurer to go over some important matters. He called the treasurer and asked him if he could reschedule their meeting for another time. That cleared his calendar for him to meet with Dan. He sensed Dan was in a crisis and that took priority over matters of business.

"Are you into hearing a confession?" Dan asked Pastor Andy the minute he entered the office.

"The confessor is in," Pastor Andy replied. "What's on your mind? And before you answer that. How is Susan?"

"Susan is going to get better," Dan answered. "She is not out of the woods, but she is beating the infection. The doctor said it was a miracle. This is really hard to talk about. I've been a fool. I'm ashamed of what I have been thinking. I have blamed God for this accident. I turned all my anger on God. I don't think God will ever forgive me!"

"And why do think God can't forgive you?" Pastor Andy asked.

"I don't deserve it!" Dan sheepishly answered.

"You're right!" Pastor Andy stated. "You are a sinner and there is nothing you can do to earn God's forgiveness. That is true for you and for everyone. But you are forgetting one very important fact. Jesus forgave you when he took upon himself the sin of the world and died for you. Dan, do you believe he did that for you?"

"Yes, I believe he died for my sins," Dan answered. "But I don't deserve it. I betrayed him. How could he…"

"Dan, you're going around in circles," Pastor Andy interrupted. "If Jesus died for you and the forgiveness of sin, that's it. I am saying this not to hurt you. I'm saying this because it is the truth. You must stop playing God like a yoyo and let God be God."

"That's just it," Dan snapped back. "I believe Jesus died for my sin and I still keep sinning. I 'm feel like garbage."

"None of us are worthy of the sacrifice God made in giving us His Son. He did this to save us from sin. You are the reason he came into the world and you are the reason he died. That's what God did. Let go of the notion you are so bad. You are no worse than Peter who betrayed him or any of the others who crucified Jesus. He said, 'Father forgive them.' Dan, do you love Jesus?"

"Yes, I love Jesus," Dan answered slowly and carefully.

"Then let Him love you," Pastor Andy stated and stopped talking. They sat there for quite awhile in silence. Finally, Pastor Andy asked, "May I pray for you?" Dan nodded agreement. They bowed their heads. "Gracious God," Pastor Andy began, "You are the creator of the universe. Your ways are not our ways, and are far beyond our understanding. Help us to trust in who You are and what You have done. May we know that the cross of Christ is our salvation. Help us to put our faith in the forgiveness You have given us by your sacrifice. Increase our faith. We hold up to You our beloved sister in Christ, Susan. May your healing power flow over and through her body. Cast this infection out of her body we ask in the name of Jesus. We pray You have mercy on her. We thank You for the doctors and nurses who are Your instruments of healing. Let Dan know, You, Lord are with him through this ordeal. In Jesus name we pray. Amen."

Dan thanked Pastor Andy and left the office. As he walked out he decided to go into the sanctuary. He stood there and looked at the altar and the big wooden cross on the wall. He sat down in a pew and stared at the old rugged cross for a long time. Then he was filled with a peace that is beyond understanding. The anger was gone. The doubt was gone. The worry was gone. He knew that he knew. It was beyond words.

As quickly as he could, he went home and gathered Troy and Dianna, and they drove to the hospital to visit Susan. When they visited Susan she was sitting up drinking some broth. She told them the doctor said she might leave the SICU in the morning. She said the broth was the most delicious thing she had tasted in a long time. This was the first thing she had eaten in many days. They had a joyful visit.

The next day when Dan visited her in the hospital, she was no longer in the SICU. She had been moved to a regular room. She was filled with hope because of what the doctor told her. "I may get to go home in a week if I keep improving," she said. "Isn't that wonderful? I'm feeling so much better. You know I was really sick?"

"You had us very worried," Dan answered. "You were about as down as a person can go, but that is behind us now. Thank God, you're doing so well. Yesterday I had a talk with Pastor Andy and it was most helpful. I want you to know I'm getting over my problems with God."

This was the news Susan was waiting to hear.

Three days later Susan found a stranger knocking at her door. "May I come in?" He asked.

Susan invited him into the room.

"My name is Frank Winters," he said. "You and I have never met. I have heard a lot about you from Jay. He's a member of my Church, where I am the senior pastor. Do you mind if we talk for a few minutes?"

"Please, sit down," Susan smiled and nodded agreement.

"Don't worry for a minute," Frank assured her. "I am not here to upset you. I heard about the accident and we have been praying for you. Please, be assured, we earnestly want you to recover completely. The good Lord is healing you in a mighty way. That has been the prophetic word we have received. But there a couple of things I think you should know. Can I confide in you?"

"Thank you for your prayers," Susan answered. "I welcome all the prayers I can get. But what do you want to confide in me? Is it about Jay?"

"This situation has put me in a difficult position," Frank continued. "Jay has been attending our church for over two, or maybe close to three years now. He has often met with me for counseling. I cannot disclose any of that information because it is strictly confidential. There are a few things that he and I have discussed that he stated he wanted me to relate to you. He is devastated by the accident you have just suffered. He regrets it happened. He regrets a number of things that have happened to you and wants your forgiveness. Please, just think about this. No need for you to answer me now. Just consider it. Forgive him for your peace of mind."

"I want to forgive him, but ..." Susan hesitated, "what exactly did he do?"

"We can't go there!" Frank sharply responded. "Let's just say, he's filled with shame and regret about things he has done. You must believe me when I tell you I am in a very troubling position having this conversation. But there is more Jay wants me to convey. He has left this country to join our mission team in the Philippines. He will be gone for quite a while. Let's just say, indefinitely. He wants you and your children to know he loves you and will pray for you. Susan, he's sincere in his concern for you."

"I believe he does love me," Susan said. "He loves Dianna and Troy in his way. The problem is he wants everything his own way. He is destructive and dangerous. I can't deal with his craziness anymore; you have no idea what he can be like."

152

"No doubt you know him far better than me," Frank said. "He has revealed sides of his personality to me that are very disturbing. I've often suggested he seek professional help, but he doesn't think he's a candidate for therapy. The Lord can deliver him from his demons. I don't want to see him locked up. The missionaries in the Philippines will bring him to the Lord for healing. He needs our prayers. He's a man of many gifts of the Spirit. Jay is also battling many demons. We've tried to exorcise them, but they've eluded us. I deeply regret this. Will you let him go in peace?"

"It sounds like I have little to say about it," Susan replied. "He's on the other side of the world and I hope he finds peace over there. Troy and Dianna need a father and I have married a good man. He will help me raise our children. I'm going to pray God will give me forgiveness in my heart for Jay. I know God can do what I'm not capable of doing."

"You have no idea what a blessing you've been to me," Frank said. "I struggled in my soul about this visit. It has been a blessing to me to meet you and have this little talk. I would like to talk more with you, but I have an appointment soon. My brother owns a roofing company and I am his chief sales representative. You know, our church can't support a full time pastor. So many of our dear people are from the streets of the city. Jay had a real passion for bringing the lost to the Lord. We will surely miss him. Praise the Lord. Susan, may our Savior watch over you and keep you safe. Bless you, and good-bye."

Susan cried for a while after Franklin left, and then she felt much better. She had peace in her heart.

Chapter 21 - The Hope

It was two months before Susan was recovered enough to return to work and by that time the school year was almost over. When she and Dan went to the church to prepare the food for the Saturday soup kitchen the volunteers at the church kitchen warmly welcomed her back. They had been following her progress and had been praying for her recovery. Even Reverend Bob gave her a hug even though he was not a demonstrative person. Billy greeted her with a package wrapped in pink paper. "Just a little sumthin made for ya while I was a prayin for ya," he said as he handed her the gift. Susan carefully unwrapped the gift and found a walnut board card with a lamb holding a staff. She looked at Billy in delight and surprise. "That thar is a picture of Jesus!" Billy exclaimed. "He be the lamb of God, ya know."

"Why, it is the most wonderful gift I ever got," Susan said. "There is a place in our front hallway where this is going to be hung. How can I ever thank you Billy? It is truly magnificent."

"Lordy, it just something I whittled for ya," Billy replied as he turned away embarrassed from the praise. "But I was a prayin the whole time I whittled that thar picture. And praise God, He was a listenin to me because here you be. Old Nick can't get ya when ya got the Lord on your side. That's the truth!"

"Billy," Susan responded, "you preach it, brother!"

When Dan and Susan went to the place to serve the food, they saw many familiar faces. Frequently they were told they had been missed. The feeling was mutual. Over time Dan and Susan had gotten to know many of the people who came for the free meal. They often sat at the tables with different people and encouraged them to tell their stories. Most often they heard about health problems like diabetes, sickle cell anemia, addictions, and mental health problems that had thrown these people into joblessness and section eight housing. The free meals were a means to survive on the meager incomes they received from social security disability. The people that most disturbed Dan were the young men who couldn't get work because they had spent time in jail. They were capable of making extravagant incomes returning to the street crimes they knew, but were trying to go straight in a world that distrusted them.

Dan recalled a strikingly handsome man one Saturday. "Man," said Vincent, "I was taking in over a thousand a day selling rock on the street. Brand new Mercedes 577, more ladies than I knew what to do with, new clothes every week, and a fat roll in my pocket was what I was when I was busted by the man. My attorney took everything I had except for the stash I gave to my Momma. Now I got nothing. I promised Momma I would go straight, but it ain't working out for me yet. Nobody wants a ex-con."

Dan and Susan knew they were merely a little band aid on the hemorrhage of poverty in the city. They were also aware there were many other people working on job training programs, halfway houses, drug treatment rehabilitation, family services, and countless other agencies to change society. They felt good about doing their small part to address the needs of the poor. There was another aspect to their work that was not often mentioned. They earnestly believed that their service in the name of Christ was a form of evangelism. Although they did not preach with words, they believed they were living and spreading the Gospel of Jesus Christ in a meaningful way. The believed they were instruments of love, hope, and faith in a cruel world. They had no patience with people who said there was nothing you could do about poverty. They felt that was either an excuse to not be involved or demonstrated a lack of compassion for the poor.

Increasingly, Dan and Susan found their real ministry was helping other churches become involved with the soup kitchen. There was a real hunger in the suburban churches to participate in hands-on mission work. Many of these groups became committed to the soup kitchen and eventually needed Dan and Susan less and less. This was the most gratifying part of the ministry. They were seeing new people becoming enthusiastically involved in ministry in the city. A side product of this was the education of the privileged suburbanites into the realities of the inner-city. Cultural, ethnic, racial, and economic barriers were being overcome every week. This was a sign of the Kingdom of God in the world.

Ahrens Furniture chain in California had an almost insatiable appetite for the furniture Dan was importing from Belize. He was constantly talking to Mr. Peters on the phone about production issues. Mr. Peters had every one of his relatives involved in the manufacture of furniture. Fortunately Mr. Peters had a large extended family. They were also hiring dozens of Belizeans to keep up with production quotas. This gave Dan the opportunity to make frequent trips to Belize. He enjoyed getting to know his new Mennonite acquaintances and the Belizean men who worked with them. He found them all to be honest and hard working. They were not interested in cutting corners in order to increase profits. Dan encouraged this commitment to quality craftsmanship. Dan was quite aware the style of furniture would eventually be copied in Asia and brought to the market. That is where he was going to be different. They would not use veneers; they would not staple joints together; they would avoid cheap man-made sheet products; and they wouldn't use softwoods stained to look like hardwood. Dan encouraged them to increase the amount of hand carving on some of the furniture which made each piece truly unique.

The consequence of the dramatic increase in Dan's business was his income grew greater than it had ever before. He and Susan decided to tithe their new business profits to the church. They also designated half of their offering to the youth mission fund they had established. Between what the youth had raised through fundraising and what Dan and Susan were contributing they had sufficient money to cover the expenses of the trip, build a new house in San Carlos, and have ample funds to provide partial scholarships for the students of San Carlos who wanted to attend high school. A new house made of concrete block cost five thousand dollars. The youth group set a goal of building two houses a year. The scholarships they gave were two hundred dollars a year which covered more than half the tuition. The cost of books, school uniforms, lunches, bus transportation, and school supplies still made it difficult for some parents to afford high school. The youth mission team set aside a fund for special cases to help these struggling families. They got advice from Harry in Iowa about the best ways to do these projects. He knew the men in the village they could trust to build the houses, and how to pay the tuition directly to the high school.

Troy and Dianna recruited many of their school friends to go on the mission. The first group of eighteen young people to go to Belize included teenagers from three different churches and two kids who didn't attend any church. They also had nine parents who accompanied the youth. For months before they left they met every other week to prepare for the trip. These meetings included Bible study, practical matters, and the geography and history of Belize. Harry had made it abundantly clear to them that the success of the mission depended upon preparation in both spiritual and practical matters.

That June when they assembled at the airport at four o'clock in the morning for their six o'clock departure, the young people were so excited they were buzzing all over the place. Most of them had never been out of the United States before. None of them had ever been on a foreign mission. Dan and Susan had their hands full getting everyone ticketed and checking their bags. On the flight to Belize half the kids slept and the other half visited each other scattered around the airplane. They were annoying the other passengers by their constant commotion. Dan repeatedly spoke to some of the worst offenders to settle down. It was hard to dampen their enthusiasm for the adventure they were just beginning. Dan and Susan organized them at the Belize airport to get through immigration and customs and then loaded into the rental vans that were waiting for them. As they drove the Northern Highway to San Carlos, they began to settle down looking out the windows of the vans at the tropical landscape.

When they arrived in San Carlos they were greeted by Pedro, Veronica, Lupe, and Hector. Veronica had prepared the Belizean specialty of rice and beans for their meal. She also included a small portion of stewed chicken on top of each plate of rice. This was a special treat often reserved for Sunday meals. Everyone enjoyed the food. The Americans had never had rice prepared with palm oil before. Veronica made the salsa less spicy this time. She did put out a plate of habaneros peppers for anyone brave enough to try one. Only a few of the boys and one girl bit into the green fire. Dan took special delight in this bit of Belizean hospitality. Susan smiled at Dan as he discretely passed on the hot peppers. Pedro ate two big habaneros like they were strawberries.

That afternoon they visited the new house under construction which they had funded for Lupe and her family. Lupe's husband, Urbano, was covering the block walls with stucco along with three other men. These men were typical of the village . They averaged a little over five feet tall , bronze skin, coal black hair, and rugged native American features. They were either of Mayan descent or a mixture of Mayan and European ancestry called Mestizo. The group of Americans watched the men patiently slap trowel loads of cement and sand mix onto the walls and spread it out in small patches. After they had an area of a couple of square feet covered they would use a long wooden trowel to smooth it further. After an area of a couple of square yards was smooth, another man would follow with a piece of flat Styrofoam and polish the wall perfectly flat. It all looked so easy. Pedro invited any of the missionaries to try it. When the brave volunteers tried putting the stucco on the wall most of it fell off. James was a six and a half foot tall high school senior and a member of the football team. He was determined to prove he could put the wet stucco on the wall like the Belizean workmen. They had trouble getting the angle and the pressure to force the stucco into the pores of the block. Pretty soon they gave up and let the Belize men get on with the work. They spent the rest of the day touring the village and meeting families.

For the next six days the group of missionaries worked as hard as they could helping to finish the house for Urbano and Lupe's family. Dan led the youth group in the mornings in helping with the finishing of the houses. James was determined to learn the craft of applying stucco to the block walls. He was always with Urbano asking questions, and trying to master the skill. They became close friends working together. James even learned how to make straight corners in cement and finish window sills at the proper angle.

Susan was the leader of the childrens Bible school program. She spent her mornings with a small group preparing for the lessons, songs, games, crafts, and snacks for the day. In the afternoons they held a five day Bible school for the children of the village which was very well attended by over one hundred children. Many of the Americans developed close friendships with some of the people in the village, especially the children. Jennifer was a red-head fifteen year old. Her skin was as pale as paper. When she got sunburned she had the most amazing freckles appear. The children loved her because she was so affectionate with them. Jennifer became the favorite of a little girl named Carmelita. This little girl had delicate Asian features and a tiny gold ring in her ear. Everywhere Jennifer went Carmelita was by her side. Jennifer told the group she wished she could take Carmelita home to America. Dan and Susan tried to facilitate these growing relationships by encouraging the youthgroup to get to know the people of the village.

On the next-to-last day of their stay in Belize they went on a tour of the Mayan ruins at Lamanani which was an hour boat ride from Orange Walk. The work they had planned to do was finished but there was something more important that happened.

The people they came to serve in Belize were helped to have a better life. They appreciated the effort the missionaries made to improve their struggle to meet the minimal needs of raising a family with little income. More importantly, the people of the village were given the hope of a better life, and they knew in their hearts that there were brothers and sisters in Christ who genuinely cared about then and came to support them. The People of the village gave the missionaries a gift that was superior to the material help the villagers received. The people of San Carlos gave their love of God and family, their contentment with the simple things of life, and their generosity of spirit to the missionaries. These qualities had a profound impact on the Americans. They were made aware of the anxiety of living in a highly materialistic society. They compared their respect for family with the Belizeans' devotion to family. They evaluated their faith in God who had filled their lives with abundance to a people who had such a strong faith in a world of scarcity. Ultimately the missionaries realized the Maya and Mestizo people of San Carlos were their spiritual brothers and sisters in Christ whom they had never known.

The morning the Americans packed up to leave San Carlos for the airport, several of the people of the village came to say goodbye. Urbano had worked all week with James at his side finishing the house. He presented James with a trowel. "You are now numero ono stucco American man," Urbano said with a big smile. James accepted the trowel with delight. Everyone cheered for his accomplishment of perseverance. There was much hugging all around. As the time came for the Americans to get in the vans and leave the village, the children began to cry and hang-on to their new American friends. As Jennifer, a high school senior from Hartwell Church, embraced a child named Carmelita, the child began weeping . "Carmelita, why are you crying?" Jennifer asked.

"You go far away," Carmelita answered through her tears, "and I never see you again. I love you Jennifer."

"I love you Carmelita," Jennifer said barely able to speak through her tears, "I will never forget you. I promise I will try to come back someday." Jennifer broke the tight embrace of the little girl and hurried onto the bus. She was silent on the long ride to the airport.

When they were waiting in the airport for the plane to load, Dianna noticed Jennifer sitting alone with a sad look on her face. She sat down next to Jennifer. "Jen, are you okay?" Dianna asked.

"I don't want to leave San Carlos," she answered. "What's going to happen to Carmelita and all the other children? I have so much, and they have nothing. It's just not fair. I want to stay in San Carlos."

"We're all feeling that way," Dianna replied, "but we can come back. We won't abandon them. Don't you think we made a difference in their lives? There is more we can do, and we will the next time. I thank God we came here." Jennifer nodded her agreement.

Chapter 22 - All the Time

Troy was usually the first one home from school unless he had soccer practice. He usually looked into the mailbox by the sidewalk to bring the mail into the house. Sometimes he just dropped the mail on the table inside the front door and didn't look through it. He rarely found mail addressed to him. This time he noticed some very pretty foreign stamps on a letter addressed to his mother so he looked at it carefully. He was surprised to discover the return address was his father's in the Philippines! He pondered opening it; but, it was addressed to his mother and he knew it would be wrong to open her mail He left it on top of the pile of mail and he decided to be around when she came home so he could satisfy his curiosity.

Mindy was leaping in circles around to take their regular walk in the woods behind the house. He and Mindy raced for the back door and Troy soon forgot about the letter.

Susan noticed the letter when she got home from teaching. She had a tiring day with her students and was thinking about relaxing for a while before she started preparing dinner. The letter caught her attention. She picked up the letter and examined it carefully front and back. She became filled with anxiety about the contents since her ex-husband Jay had not been heard from in almost a year since he left for the Philippines. Carefully she opened the envelope and unfolded the letter. Jay wrote, greeting her and the children, and then got right to the point. He had married a Philippine woman who was a widow with five children. He was helping to plant new churches. He was having great success evangelizing and many people received Christ as a result. He now knew that God had called him to do this work, and he was being filled with many gifts of the Spirit. They had a healing ministry and many miracles happened bring new converts into the church. He concluded the letter with an assurance he was praying for them and asked God to bless them. Susan reread the letter several times before she put it down.

Just when she had fully grasped the importance of the events described in the letter, Troy came bounding into the room followed by Mindy. "Hey Mom!" he shouted, "Mindy found a turtle in our backyard. Do you want to see it?" And then he noticed the letter in Susan's hand and the envelope in her lap. "Did you read Dad's letter?" he asked. "What'd he say? Can I read it?"

It's good news!" Susan said. "It's all good. Why don't you just read it yourself." She handed the letter to Troy.

After he finished reading the letter, he asked Susan fearfully, "Do you think he will stay in the Philippines with his new family?"

That is what I think will happen because he has found his calling there," Susan answered. "Maybe someday they will come to the States; but, who knows what will happen? Now you have five new brothers and sisters on the other side of the world. That's exciting."

"Yah, I guess." Troy said flatly. "Well we're going to see if the turtle has stuck his head out. He's in the backyard."

Dianna came home a short while later and Susan gave her the letter to read. She was very interested in her father's new wife and family. She asked Susan many questions about Jay's new family that Susan was unable to answer. Finally, in response to Dianna's questions, Susan said, "The return address is on the envelope. Why don't you write him and ask him? I bet he would be thrilled to hear from you. Tell him about the things you've been doing. He would love to hear about your life."

Dan was the last to read the letter. He and Susan talked about it for some time. They were so happy Jay had seemed to find a place where he could be fulfilled. They hoped this meant he had found his purpose in life and stop threatening them. By the time they exhausted the subject it was after six o'clock and they had forgotten bout dinner. Dan suggested they all go out to eat at their favorite Italian restaurant. Susan was delighted with the suggestion. This was in informal celebration of new life for everyone.

The difference the news from Jay made in the lives of Susan, Dan, Troy, and Dianna was subtle, but profound. By the grace of God they had sincerely prayed for Jay and wished him well when he went to the Philippines. They harbored no resentment towards him, but they were also concerned that he would return to interfere in their lives. Since he had not only remarried, but had also found his calling as an evangelist made them happy for him and relieved that God had found a place for him in the world. They could go in with their lives without the looming fear of Jay menacing them.

Dan continued attending the men's support group - the one he had been attending since the beginning of his journey in the Christian faith. There were several topics that came up with a strange regularity. These were issues that could never be completely resolved. They often discussed how to be an authentic follower of Jesus. Each individual in the group occasionally had doubts if they were doing enough in their Christian faith. They would talk about what they were doing and what opportunities they had to do more.

The fact that they asked the question about their commitment was a healthy indication of their genuine attachment to Jesus. How to balance the demands of making a living, attending to the needs of family, and involvements in ministry and missions was never easy to accomplish completely.

Another issue that was prominently wrestled with was the mystery of women. They all agreed that they were doing the best they could to met the emotional needs of their wives or significant others, but they often felt disappointed in the results. They frequently referred to 1 Corinthians 13 as the standard of love. They had all heard this frequently at weddings, and they believed it. Living perfectly the words of Saint Paul on the meaning of love was difficult, if not impossible. They agreed they were imperfect people in relationship with imperfect people so it was not possible to have a relationship free from problems. How to find complete happiness without strife eluded them. So they struggled seeking ways they could change their behavior to satisfy the needs of their partners. They concluded they had little chance of changing the behavior of their partners, so they were responsible for adjusting their thinking.

A third issue had to do with the Christ's church that they could never successfully come to any conclusions about. The men saw the role of the church in society decline. The world increasingly viewed the religion as irrelevant, foolish or hypocritical. The church like every other institution was flawed by the people who comprise it. Like the law, medicine, education, industry, rocket science, and every other complex structure populated with humans, they decided the church needs constant reform. What specific changed could be made are always controversial, and the subject of much argument within the structure. The prevailing attitude amongst so many church critics is passivity is preferable to the hard work of reformation. In the support group there was a general consensus to work within the church to make it more relevant and responsive to the contemporary culture. The difficulty was the high regard so many of them had for the traditions that they knew were becoming outdated. There are generational clashes in the changes that must take place. The group members know it's very painful to rearrange sacred liturgy and sacred space. This group of men wavered between the necessities of dramatic change versus incremental change without ever deciding which as best.

Dan and Susan had a similar theological understanding of their faith which bonded them together and helped them find solutions to any situation that arose. They both knew Jesus Christ with whom they stayed in conversation in their daily lives. In addition to knowing the historical Jesus described in the Gospels, they knew the living Christ. They used their imagination to hear him speak to them by studying through others persons of faith. It was the preaching of their pastor, the men and women of their church, Christian writers, and trusted brothers and sisters in the faith that many times spoke to them and the Spirit of Christ was speaking to them. Dan and Susan prayed in many different ways, but they also practiced listening for God's voice. They both new it required practice and patience, but the small still voice of God can be heard in the heart and mind of the one who seeks it. Dan and Susan would sometimes say as a preface to a statement, "I believe God is telling me too..." They did not use this phrase with anyone they were not intimately connected with. They were aware some people would be suspicious of someone who claimed God spoke to them for they were also aware that there are many voices in one's mind, and it takes careful discernment to be certain one is listening to God and not to a deceiving voice. By their intimate relationship and knowledge for Jesus Christ, they carefully compared what they were hearing with what Jesus said and did in the gospels. That is the primary way they tested the spirits.

Hartwell Church was their spiritual home. They loved the members of the congregation. As they became more involved with various ministries of the church, they learned more about different individuals. It wasn't until they spent time with people that they really began to appreciate them. They were surprised at the depth of struggle many people had been through and some were going through. They both adored Jane, who was a retired nurse with a withered leg and an infectious laugh. They learned about her battle with polio as a teenager and working her way through college as a waitress. Jan had buried three husbands and always put everyone's needs ahead of her own. They loved Nick, the teenager, who came from an abusive home as was living with this grandparents. Nick volunteered for any job without being asked. It was hard to comprehend how Nick was so willing to help when he has been so mistreated. They didn't know the specifics about the generosity of Tom Johansen, but they suspected he was the one who gave the big amounts when programs were underfunded. The pastor never revealed it was Tom; but, when he said thanks to the generosity of an anonymous donor some people were sure it was Tom. Tom never talked about his giving and never made demands upon the church. Dan and Susan had a special love for Ruth who complained about most everything. They knew Ruth was a widow whose deceased husband was an alcoholic. She was lonely and craved attention, so she had a comment about everything. They didn't take her continuous critical commentary seriously, and they tried to give her affirmation for all the work she did in the kitchen at the church. She practically ran the kitchen as if it was her kingdom. There were so many interesting characters in the congregation once you took the time to get to know them. Dan and

Susan grew more and more in love with this interesting assortment of people.

Susan noticed a change in Dan as time went by. When she met him she knew he was devoted to his business of importing furniture. He was at times frantic about making a sale to a new client. He was very moody when a shipment was late and the customer was pressuring him to expedite the shipment. As the business grew, Dan became less emotional about the inevitable problems and highs and lows in sales. She had worried when he started making a lot more money because she was afraid he would become consumed by success. The fact was Dan became less worried about is business the better he did. He was becoming more confident in his abilities as a businessman and, more importantly, he was trusting in God to help him, to relieve his worries, and believing God was in control of everything. Dan prayed about his business decisions and handed the outcome over to God. It worked for him. This change made Dan more present to his family and more fun to be with.

Susan had a lot of well earned distrust of men from her previous marriage experience. This came out in many little ways that hurt her relationship with Dan. She was critical of him when it was unnecessary and insecure about his motives when his intentions were beyond reproach. For Dan, these were like little cuts that accumulated over time. It was going to take Susan years to heal her insecurity and truly learn to trust Dan. She had been forced to build a wall of defenses around herself and not be vulnerable to the harm her former husband could do. It is very difficult to let the armor down once it has become habitual. There were times when Susan realized she was protecting herself where there was no threat. Slowly and cautiously she gained more insight into her automatic responses and saw them for what they were. It is only through the self-awareness that God gave her that she was able to redo the old patterns of behavior. Susan was in the process of remaking herself bit by bit. The walls began to come down.

Troy became more confident because he had a role model in Dan who was accepting of him and his interests. This was the opposite of his father who demanded perfection and subordination. Troy was not afraid of Dan. He respected him and did not have to put their relationship to the test as a rebellious teenager. He flourished playing soccer and began to show a strong interest in architecture which Dan encouraged.

Dianna had a passion for skating and was also an excellent student. She was not very interested in dating. She kept her social life confined to friendships which were involvements with both sexes. She was determined to get into an Ivy League University and focused her energy into excelling in academics. When Dan had opportunities he took Dianna to visit places like Yale, Harvard or Princeton.

Dianna had hoped she was destined to be a world class figure skater. During a practice in the summer of her senior year of high school she shattered her knee attempting a triple jump. Not only did this remove her from further completion for six months, but this was an injury that destroyed any hope of successfully competing on the level she had hoped of attaining, Diana went through a serious period of severe depression. "Why did God let me work so hard," she asked repeatedly, "just to let me break my knee? How could this happen?"

No one could console her. Dan and Susan had a difficult time getting her to return to church after she recovered sufficiently to walk. "What difference does it make whether I go to church of not?" She explained. "God doesn't care!" It wasn't until Dianna had a visit from Julie, a close friend, who had a brother with Down's Syndrome that something changed. Julie talked to Dianna about God's love for her brother and her brother's faith in God.

"God loves my brother, and he loves God," Julie said. "He is perfect in God's eyes. I don't feel sorry for my brother. God has a good purpose for his life. Do you think he is less important because he is different than other people?"

"I guess I have just been feeling sorry for myself," Dianna said. "Maybe it's time to stop blaming God?"

"Dianna, God is good all the time," Julie replied. "You have your whole life ahead of you, and God has a good purpose for your life too."

Over time she not only regained her faith but it grew stronger as a result of the crisis she has suffered. Every time she had a difficult situation she learned to not blame God, instead she relied on God for the wisdom and the perseverance to overcome the challenge she was facing. Her faith became a source of strength to her family and friends. Too often when people need the good gifts that God wants to give us we turn away from God and lose the opportunity to overcome adversity.

Dan and Susan did not have a perfect marriage because they are not perfect people. Because of the disappointment and caution they felt about trusting a member of the opposite sex they had issues between them. Trust is only developed over time and that is where they had much room to grow. Trusting another human being and trusting God are interrelated. Love is being vulnerable and trusting.

Faith is loving and trusting God. One learns in our relationships in this world. Everyone has been betrayed and exploited which makes trust difficult. This is what Dan and Susan had to overcome. But it is better to risk love than to never really allow it to flourish. Life is how we have loved. God is love.

Dan, Susan, Dianna, and Troy had an abiding faith that God was good all the time. They did believe God had a good purpose for those who loved God. They knew they would face many trials and temptations, but they were equipped, by the grace of God, to handle anything. They knew God watched over them and were protected with their angels.

Printed in Great Britain
by Amazon

ISBN 9781505205978